Praise for the novels
author

Dance of Desire
"On a scale of 1-5 stars, this is definitely a 6 star book! . . . Don't miss this one!"—6 stars, *Affaire de Coeur* Magazine

My Lady's Treasure
"Filled with lively characters, a strong, suspenseful plot and a myriad of romantic scenes *My Lady's Treasure* is a powerful, poignant tale that will keep readers turning pages until the very end."—5 stars and Reviewer's Choice Award, The Road to Romance

A Knight's Vengeance
"Kean (*Dance of Desire*) delivers rich local color and sparkling romantic tension in this fast-paced medieval revenge plot."—*Publishers Weekly*

A Knight's Reward
"Ms. Kean has done it again with her talent to capture the reader's attention with all the elements of a must-read. The opening pages are filled with a wonderful tension that sets the stage for a great story."—Fresh Fiction

A Knight's Temptation
"...an entertaining medieval romance brimming with sass, action, adventure, and lots of sexual chemistry."—*Booklist*

A Knight's Persuasion
"...stirring adventure, superb characters, and enticing heroes. Ms. Kean continues to snag the reader with her fast-paced tales of heroic knights."—4-1/2 stars, *Affaire de Coeur* Magazine

Books by Catherine Kean

A Knight and His Rose
A Knight to Remember (Novella)
A Legendary Love (Novella)
Bound by His Kiss (Novella)
Dance of Desire
Her Gallant Knight (Novella)
My Lady's Treasure
One Knight in the Forest (Novella)
One Knight Under the Mistletoe (Novella)
One Knight's Kiss (Novella)
That Knight by the Sea (Novella)

<u>Lost Riches</u> Series
A Knight's Desire (Book 1)
An Outlaw's Desire (Book 2)

<u>Knight's Series</u> Novels
A Knight's Vengeance (Book 1)
A Knight's Reward (Book 2)
A Knight's Temptation (Book 3)
A Knight's Persuasion (Book 4)
A Knight's Seduction (Book 5)
A Knight's Redemption (Book 6)

<u>Boxed Sets</u>
The Knight's Series: Books 1-5

<u>Paranormal Romances</u>
A Witch in Time
Hot Magic

A Knight's Desire

Book 1 of the *Lost Riches* Series

by

Catherine Kean

Cover Art © 2021 by Cora Graphics

Cover Images © Depositphotos.com and TheKillionGroupImages.com.

ISBN: 9781724104441

Also available in eBook.
ASIN: B07HNJRTXQ

Catherine Kean
P.O. Box 917624
Longwood, FL 32791-7624
www.catherinekean.com

Chapter One

The town of Clipston
Warwickshire, England
Early August, 1192

L ady Rosetta Montgomery tightly gripped the reins of her white mare. Raising her veiled head, she strained to hear over the merry melody of flutes, pipes, and a tabor played by the musicians walking ahead of her horse. Step by step, the musicians led her and her three armed guards—two in front and one behind—through the crowded streets toward the church in the town square. Moments from now, on the church's sun-drenched portico, she would be joined in holy matrimony to her dear friend, Lord Edric Sherborne.

Yet, barely audible over the music, she could hear a distant thundering sound: the pounding of a horse's hooves?

If only there wasn't such a cacophony around her. Cheering, clapping peasants and townspeople crowded in along both sides of the narrow street lined with two-story wattle-and-daub homes. The folk, excited by their lord's nuptials, had come out to honor her processional horseback ride from Millenstowe Keep, where she'd been born and had lived with her parents until this very day.

Once married, she'd leave with Edric for her new home: Wallensford Keep, which he'd inherited not long ago upon his father's death. There, they'd celebrate their wedding with a feast and celebrations befitting a union of two well-respected noble families. Regret wove through Rosetta, for this journey was her last as an unwed maiden. Tonight, she'd lie with Edric in his solar, and mayhap even conceive his heir.

She tried to listen for the hoof beats again, but peasants, their gazes filled with awe, reached out to touch the hem of her cloak.

"Stand back. Do not try to touch her ladyship," her guards commanded.

"Milady!" cried an older woman in the crowd, happy tears streaming down her wrinkled face. "Ye are the most beautiful bride."

Beneath the veil held in place on her head by a gold circlet—a betrothal gift from Edric—Rosetta forced a smile and waved to the throng. These would be her folk too, once she became Lady Sherborne.

Convince all who gaze upon you that you are a joyful bride, a voice inside her coaxed. *'Tis your noble duty. Moreover, Norman blood runs in your veins; your ancestors were champions who arrived on English shores years ago to fight alongside William the Conqueror. Show these people that in your own way, you are as strong as a warrior.*

Those words could have been spoken by her mother, Odelia, who'd fiercely clung to her Norman heritage until the crown had arranged her marriage to an equally headstrong Saxon lord by the name of Milton Montgomery. Her parents had been strangers to one another when they'd wed, but as the weeks had passed, they had fallen in love. Twenty years later, their marriage was still a happy one. The sapphire blue cloak Rosetta wore, embroidered in gold thread, was the same garment her mother had worn on her wedding day.

Unlike her mother, Rosetta's marriage hadn't been arranged by the crown. She'd accepted Edric's proposal—his third time asking her—because his estate bordered her sire's for several leagues, and she'd known Edric since childhood. Their years of friendship would provide the foundation for a good marriage, and in time, she'd grow to love Edric, as her parents had grown to cherish one another.

She'd never love Edric, though, the way she'd loved their childhood friend, Lord Ashton Blakeley—as if he'd been an integral part of her soul.

As she continued to wave, Rosetta tamped down the anguish that bloomed whenever she thought of Ash. He didn't want her. He hadn't answered her letters. She hadn't seen him in years, even though she'd heard that he'd returned to England weeks ago.

Today she'd move on with her life—

Again, over the music and cheering, she caught the thunder of hoof beats. The sound was louder now.

Why would anyone ride through the town at a gallop, especially when the streets were full of people? Had something happened at one of the castles that required her father or Edric to be notified right away? Rosetta started to turn in the saddle, to look behind her, but three little girls, grinning as if they offered her priceless jewels, ran alongside her horse and offered her their scraggly bouquets of dandelions, daisies, and cornflowers. Murmuring her thanks, she leaned down, accepted the gifts, and tucked them in front of her saddle for safekeeping.

As she smoothed her cloak over the light-copper-colored silk of her gown, the clatter of hooves grew closer. Behind Rosetta, a woman screamed. More frantic cries erupted, accompanied by the panicked sounds of folk scrambling to get out of the way.

The musicians' vibrant melody faltered and then died.

"What is happening?" Rosetta asked, swiveling to glance behind her. Her eyes widened.

A man on a huge, black horse raced toward her. The

rider's black cape billowed out behind him, and spurs glinted at the heels of his black boots. He wore an older-style iron helm with eye slits and a nasal guard that covered all but the lower third of his face.

Judging by the breadth of his shoulders, and the ease with which he rode, he was a trained warrior—and determined that no one would stand in his way.

"Milady, move into that alley. Wait for us there," one of her men-at-arms said, gesturing to the street opening to the left a short distance ahead. He and his fellow guard moved to intercept the rider, while the third man-at-arms strode alongside her as she guided her mare toward the alley.

She glanced over her shoulder, to see the two guards standing in the middle of the street.

One of them raised his hand, palm outward. "Hold," he shouted.

The rider didn't slow his horse.

Why didn't the horseman obey? The embroidered crest on the guards' surcoats identified them as Edric's men. Her future husband's estate included Clipston and the surrounding lands for several leagues. The rider was duty-bound to halt as commanded, but he clearly didn't respect the authority of Edric's guards.

Was the horseman an enemy of her future husband's, then?

She sensed the rider's stare slide from the men-at-arms to her. Dread formed an icy knot in the pit of her stomach.

He'd come for *her*.

She'd heard stories of brides being abducted on their wedding days and held for ransom—or worse—but such things never happened in this part of Warwickshire.

Until now?

Shock and panic swirled up inside her. "Oh, God," she whispered. Rosetta nudged the heels of her embroidered shoes into her mare's side, urging the horse to a trot.

"Hold!" the guard standing in the street shouted again. With a harsh cry, the rider bore down on him, slowing his mount only at the last moment. As the guard drew his sword, the horseman kicked him hard in the middle of his chest. Gasping, the guard staggered sideways, colliding with several frightened townsfolk and falling to the ground.

The second man-at-arms, sword drawn, lunged at the rider. Steel glinted as the horseman drew his broadsword and met the guard's attack, delivering powerful strikes that forced the soldier back. Seizing an opportunity, the rider kicked out, catching the man-at-arms in the shoulder and sending him reeling. His head knocked against a wall, and he crumpled, unconscious.

The remaining guard moved between Rosetta and the rider.

The entrance to the alley loomed ahead. As the sound of pounding hooves rang in her ears, she kicked her heels hard into her mare's side. The horse launched into a gallop.

"Milady," the guard cried, a clear warning to halt, but she ignored it. She had to get away. Whatever the man on the black horse wanted, whatever grievance he had with Edric, she wasn't going to be a part of it.

Grayed shadows swallowed Rosetta as her mare raced down the alley. The stench of rotting vegetables, moldy crates, and stagnant puddles rose from the ground, and her eyes watered as she fought not to cough. Sweat gathered on her forehead beneath the veil, causing the fabric to cling to her skin. She must find her way to the town square. If she could reach the church where Edric, her parents, and all of their friends were waiting, she would be safe. The rider would be captured and arrested for his recklessness.

The clatter of hoof beats echoed off the walls behind her. The horseman had entered the alley.

Anger simmered in her veins, along with the urge to escape. This was her wedding day. How dare this rider use such an occasion—indeed, try to use *her*—to exact some kind of vengeance against Edric? Whoever this horseman was, he would pay for his folly.

The shadows gave way to sunlight, as the alley opened onto another street. She slowed her mare a fraction, urging it to take the sharp right turn.

"Rosetta," the rider yelled, his voice as rough as grating stone.

Shock jolted through her. *He hadn't called her 'milady'. He knew her given name.*

How? She didn't recognize his voice, and yet, somehow, there was something oddly familiar about it. Once he was captured, she'd demand to know his identity.

The alley ahead was littered with mounds of muck and piles of broken tiles. As her mare galloped through the sludge, flies swarmed up and buzzed around Rosetta. Loosening one hand from the reins, she swatted the insects away, while trying to see the route ahead.

The hammering of hooves was as loud as her heartbeat. The horseman was gaining on her.

"Ha!" she cried, urging her mare on. "Ha!"

A child darted out of a doorway ahead: A little boy, holding a ball.

"Oh, mercy," Rosetta shrieked. Her mare startled and whinnied, a frantic sound. The horse flailed its head, while it skidded in the muck, trying to halt.

Rosetta lost her balance. She careened sideways, the weight of her cloak and costly silk gown pulling her toward the ground. Desperately, she grabbed for her mare's saddle, her nails clawing at the leather, but her fingers couldn't get a firm grip. Flowers tumbled, falling onto her as she landed on her back in a pile of filth. Her circlet and veil fell from her head and landed in the muck beside her.

Gasping for breath, she pushed up on her arms and looked for the child. He'd escaped harm and stood pressed against the wall, near her winded mare.

Rosetta struggled to stand, but the slick filth squelched beneath her, denying her any solid footing.

The rider was upon her.

In one effortless movement, he slid from his saddle. His boots sloshed in the grime, and then, tall and imposing, he was looming over her.

Her hands fisted into the cold muck, readying to hurl some at him. "Leave me be!" she cried.

"I cannot," he rasped.

"Who are you? What do you *want?*" She hated that her voice shook, but she had a right to know his name and why he was pursuing her.

"Trust me," he ground out, "all will be explained later."

"I want explanations now."

Men's voices carried on the breeze. Her guards were searching for her. Hope warmed her, even as she resolved to keep the rider talking. If she could delay him, her guards would find them. He was at a disadvantage now, being on foot.

The horseman's head lifted, as though he had also heard the voices. Stretching out his gloved hand to her, he said, "Come."

"Never." She scooted backward, splattering more filth on her garments.

"You will come with me, Rosetta. *Now.*"

Her anger flared. Unless he was a nobleman, he had no right to address her by her first name. If he *was* a nobleman, he was behaving in a most shameful and dishonorable manner. "If warn you, you *dare* try to touch me—"

A hissed breath parted his lips. He reached down to

grab her arm.

She threw a fistful of grime in his face. It splattered on his helm, and as he cursed and wiped it away, she shoved to her feet.

She was almost standing, but her leather shoes skidded in the filth. The alley spun around her, and she fell, landing on a heap of broken tiles.

Pain splintered through her head.

All went black.

A cry burning in his throat, Lord Ashton Blakely lunged for Rosetta, trying to break her fall. His right boot slipped, and he fought to stay upright, even as she fell hard on the mound of tiles. Her body went limp, and her eyelids fluttered closed.

"Briar Rose," he whispered, reaching her side.

Ash crouched beside her, fear lancing through him. His damaged hands ached from wielding his sword and gripping his destrier's reins, but he refused to heed his own discomfort. Rosetta was most important now.

Ah, God, he'd never meant for her to be hurt. He'd expected her panic and outrage. After all, he hadn't had the chance to reintroduce himself to her; 'twas best—safest—to keep his features concealed while he was in Clipston. Once they'd left the town far behind, he'd intended to remove the helm. When she was secured within his castle's walls, he'd planned to explain the reasons for his actions. Never, at any point in his careful planning, had he anticipated that she'd be wounded.

With gentle fingers, he turned her head sideways, his heart constricting at the pale color of her face. He couldn't see any blood, but that didn't mean she was unharmed.

"Rosetta," he said again, gently shaking her. With anger flashing in her blue eyes, and her cheeks pink with fury, she'd been a magnificent creature, a warrior maiden. Pale and unresponsive as she was now, she seemed fragile and vulnerable—the way she'd looked when he'd ridden off with Edric for the great City of London, to join King Richard's Crusade.

Ash tamped down the anger that burned whenever he thought of Edric, as shouts and raised voices carried to him again. Edric's soldiers were getting closer. Soon, they'd be upon him, and no way in hellfire was he going to be caught.

He drew Rosetta into his arms. Her head lolled, and pins fell from her blonde hair that had been braided and neatly coiled around her head. He carefully turned her so that her cheek rested against his left shoulder. After snatching up her mud-covered circlet and veil, and shoving them into the leather bag tied to his sword belt, he rose and carried her to his destrier.

The little boy, still pressed back against the wall, watched him.

He swung up onto his horse, adjusting Rosetta so that she sat sideways in his lap, her face still pressed against him. Her exquisite cloak and silk gown were badly soiled, but there was naught he could do about the muck now. Snatching up his horse's reins, he nudged his mount toward the boy, who shrank back, as if he wanted to blend into the shadows.

Ash reached into his bag again and tossed the child a few pieces of silver. Edric's men likely wouldn't pay much heed to information provided by a child, but Ash still wanted to ensure the boy's silence. "Do not tell anyone what you just saw. Agreed?"

Nodding, the boy picked up the coins.

Spurring his horse forward, Ash drew up alongside Rosetta's mare and smacked it on the hindquarters. The horse bolted, its reins dangling. Edric's men would waste good time chasing the mare and searching the streets for Rosetta, only to finally realize that the lady was missing.

Drawing Rosetta in closer, Ash nudged his destrier to a canter. At the next intersecting of streets, he turned his horse toward the outskirts of the town, where the lanes were quiet. Most of the townsfolk were still gathered along the route to the church, hoping to catch a glimpse of the woman who was to become their lord's wife. Those who'd witnessed Ash attack her guards and pursue her were likely helping to search for both him and her.

Ash looked down at Rosetta, cradled in his arms, and his mouth curled into a smile.

At last, just as he'd promised her long ago, Rosetta was *his*.

Chapter Two

Rosetta woke slowly. Her muzzy head throbbed. Mother Mary, she'd had the oddest dream. In it, she had been riding sideways upon a horse, looking up at Ash—only he wasn't the Ash she knew, because the man who had returned her stare had a hideous scar slashing across his forehead and down into his left eyebrow. She must have dreamed of Ash because she'd thought of him on the way to the church…and yet, why could she not remember the wedding ceremony?

Her eyes still closed, she moaned, for she felt truly wretched. Her whole body ached.

She lifted a hand to rub her brow. A rustling noise accompanied the movement: the sound of shifting cloth. As her senses sharpened, she realized she was lying on her back, her head on a pillow. She must be in a bed. That would explain the soft fabric, infused with the faint fragrance of soap, that brushed her skin; the linen sheets had been recently washed.

There was another, earthier smell, too: a distinctly masculine scent.

She must be in the solar at Wallensford Keep. Surely, though, she'd remember at least something of her wedding night with Edric? She'd overheard several maids gossiping about how pleasurable 'twas to couple with men, especially those with lusty appetites and experience in the bed chamber, but Rosetta certainly didn't recall any moments of glorious pleasure.

The last things she remembered were being chased by the rider and falling in the alley—

Alarm raced through her. She opened her eyes to see rough-hewn beams overhead. 'Twas not a ceiling she recognized.

"'Tis good to see you awake, milady. How are you feeling?"

Turning her head on the pillow, Rosetta found a chestnut-haired young woman sitting in a carved oak chair pushed up to the bedside. Pain shot through Rosetta's head, and she winced, while fighting the sickening lurch of her stomach.

Her smile kind and encouraging, the woman rose. "I will tell his lordship. He wanted to know the moment you woke."

"His lordship?" Rosetta hoped that she meant Edric, or her father, or one of her other relatives who could tell her how she'd come to be in this place. Closing her eyes while she rubbed her forehead, she said, "Please. Where—?"

A *click* told her the woman had hurried out the door.

Rosetta sighed, for she could barely think past the hammering in her skull, but she must determine what had happened since she'd fallen and lost consciousness. Mayhap seeing more of the chamber would prod her memories and help answer some of her questions.

Slowly, carefully, she eased herself up to sitting. As the bedding fell to her lap, she realized she wore only a linen chemise. Judging by the coarse weave of the fabric and lack of embroidery, 'twas not one of her own.

Rosetta glanced about the chamber, her gaze

skimming from the iron-bound wooden door across from the bed to the long oak trestle table set with candles and other items that was pushed against the opposite wall. A fire burned in the hearth, and a thick Eastern-style rug covered the floorboards. Two linen chests rested against the right wall, and oak tables, also set with candles, flanked each side of the bed. She most certainly had never been in this chamber before, and all of the furnishings were unfamiliar.

Panic rose, forming a crushing tightness in her breast, but fretting would solve naught. She must remain strong and figure out what was going on.

While she didn't see her wedding garments and shoes in the room, at least she hadn't lost her pearl and emerald betrothal ring, which glinted on her left hand. Was her circlet still lying with her veil in the muddy alley? Edric would be upset if she had lost his costly gift.

Panic threatened to well again, but she fought for calm. Her circlet could well be with her garments and shoes, which had been handed over to servants to be cleaned. The items had, after all, been thoroughly filthy. Her skin was clean, and so was her hair, falling loose about her shoulders, which meant someone had washed off the filth from the alley. Had the young woman who'd sat beside the bed done so?

When she returned, Rosetta must ask her what had happened to her belongings. Moreover, Rosetta dearly wanted to know the name of this place where she'd been brought.

The chamber door swung inward.

"You are back," Rosetta said. "Thank g—" The rest of her words froze in her mouth.

A man walked through the doorway. A tall, well-muscled warrior dressed all in black, from his belted tunic to his woolen hose and knee-high black boots: the rider from Clipston.

As he entered, he set an object down on the trestle table: her circlet.

She glanced back up at him, and her gaze riveted to his face. Wavy, dark brown hair fell to his shoulders and framed a visage bronzed by the sun. 'Twas a handsome face, apart from the puckered red scar that slashed across his forehead and spliced downward through his left eyebrow. The wound had very nearly taken his eye.

This was the man from her dream.

She knew, without the slightest doubt, that he was once the Ash she had loved.

Years ago, Rosetta had memorized every part of his beautiful face with her fingers and lips. She'd offered him her heart, her soul, without the slightest reservation. She'd loved him with a passion that had nigh consumed her, and in memory of what they had shared, a cherished part of who she was would always belong to him.

That he had been so disfigured made her want to weep. She wouldn't, though. Not in front of this man, this stranger, whose aura of sheer, unbridled boldness made her clutch the bedding tightly to her bosom.

Her gaze locked with eyes the hue of polished oak.

"Ash," she whispered.

He held Rosetta's stare, watched as color spread across her face and down the smooth column of her throat. He followed the redness as far as he could, but nowhere near as far as he wanted. Her hands were pinning the blankets to her chest.

He'd always loved the way she blushed. Her skin would go from a pale cream to the pink of a wild rose. Her blushing always made her blue eyes look exceptionally bright. Years ago, he'd struggled to describe the exact color of her eyes, but after going on Crusade, he knew: They were the hue of the Mediterranean Sea.

Turning slightly, he pushed the solar door closed. It shut with a muffled *thud*, and she flinched. While he understood her nervous reaction, it still made his heart twist in his chest.

Ash crossed to the side of the bed, his footfalls loud on the planks in the quiet room. Her eyes widened, disquiet glimmering in their depths before she gathered her emotions and cool determination replaced all trace of unease.

He halted beside the bed, the carved chair within arm's reach. His gloved hands curled as she continued to hold his gaze. He had to admire her courage; most women couldn't bear to look at him with his ugly scar. Truth be told, he could barely stand to see his own reflection.

Silence persisted, each passing moment making the air between them thicker, heavier with the weight of past memories. He indulged his ravenous curiosity, allowed his gaze to wander over her, to savor what naked skin he could see and to acknowledge the beautiful woman she'd become. His gaze snagged on the ring on her left hand—a gaudy ornament for a woman with such delicate hands—and then moved on.

Her tresses were still the color of pure gold limned by sunshine. How keenly he remembered the silken glide of her hair as he'd plunged his hands into it to hold her head still for his kiss. How easily he recalled the taste of her lips, as sweet and ripe as the blackberries they'd picked together and feasted on while lying on a blanket down by the creek on her father's lands. How desperately Ash wanted to feel again the soft warmth of her skin beneath his fingertips, but that pleasure was forever denied to him now; he never removed his gloves, except when he was alone. Most of the time, not even then.

"Why do I remember you…as if from a dream?" she finally asked, her voice little more than a whisper.

"A good dream?" He'd secretly hoped that she would still be dreaming about him after all these years. Mayhap she'd be more receptive to what he had to reveal to her than he'd expected.

Rosetta frowned. "We were on a horse—"

"Ah. You woke during our ride here, not long after we left Clipston. When you saw me—rather, saw my scar—you fainted."

She looked down at the bedding; she clearly didn't like that she had swooned. "Why does your voice sound different?"

"My throat was damaged after I was wounded in the East."

She was clearly curious about what had befallen him, but her frosty resolve returned. "What do you want, Ash?"

A brittle laugh broke from him. "*That* is all you have to say to me, after not seeing me for years?"

Her lips flattened, a clear attempt to stop them from trembling. "What else would I say? You stopped my wedding. There must be a reason why you were so exceedingly bold. If not, I warn you, my father and Edric will—"

"There is a very good reason. Indeed, more than one."

She studied him warily.

"I will tell you all, but not just yet."

An indignant huff broke from her. "Why must you be so secretive? Why bother to ride back into my life *today*? You have had weeks to see me or get in touch with me if you wanted. When I heard you had returned to England, I wrote to you. Did you not get my letters? You never replied."

A muscle ticked in his jaw. He'd received her letters.

They were carefully stowed in one of his linen chests, just a few steps away, but a great many urgent matters had demanded his time and focus once he'd landed on English soil. He'd spent most of the past weeks in London, or traveling to meet with contacts recommended by the crown, or at his late brother's castle, not here at Damsley Keep. Even if he had found a moment to write to her, he had trouble holding a quill now; his handwriting was nigh illegible.

"You never even visited Millenstowe Keep," she pressed.

"I had other responsibilities." Including the one he'd send out to the tiltyards to practice his archery.

"After refusing to see or speak to me for years, you then attempt to kidnap me—"

"Nay, I did not attempt. I *did* kidnap you, Briar Rose."

Her eyes hardened. "Do not call me that."

"What? Briar Rose?"

Anguish flickered across her fine-boned features before her expression once again darkened with barely repressed anger. "Do not mock me."

"I am not—"

"You *are*. You know what that endearment once meant to me."

Regret pierced the iron shield around his heart. The endearment had been precious to him, too. He crushed the inconvenient emotion.

"Where have you brought me?" she demanded. "Am I at Damsley Keep?"

"You are."

Her eyes flashed. "A fortress ceded to you by the King, if I remember correctly."

"Aye."

"A reward for all of your honorable victories in battle

while on Crusade."

Ignoring the bite in her voice, Ash sat in the chair; it creaked as he stretched his long legs out in front of him and crossed them at the ankles. She was waiting for him to reply, and he let her wait while his gaze skimmed up the slender, bare length of her arm to her face. "This castle was indeed a reward—"

"And yet, you are willing to risk the crown's disfavor by abducting the intended of one of your peers, on the day of her wedding no less?"

Risk the King's disfavor? Laughter welled in Ash's throat, but he swallowed it down. What he did for King Richard wasn't to be discussed with anyone except those trusted few within the crown council in London, as well as several other men the King had told Ash he could rely upon when needed.

Ash crossed his arms, the indolent posture drawing her gaze to his chest before she swiftly looked away. "Well?" Rosetta said.

"I am not concerned about reprisal from the King."

Shock registered in her eyes. "Why not?"

He shrugged. "Because…"

"Because? 'Tis all you can say?"

He smiled, a wry tilt of his mouth. "'Tis all I *care* to say."

Rosetta shook her head. She looked drawn and weary, and with a pang of concern, he reminded himself to have her head wound examined again. Earlier, while she'd slept, the castle healer had found a lump on the right side of head and bruises on her right arm and hip, but she had assured Ash that Rosetta would be all right after a good rest. He truly hoped so.

Rosetta winced as she rubbed her brow. "Edric will find out what you have done—"

Edric. His lip curling, Ash growled, "I expect so."

"He will bring his men-at-arms to your castle gates. Is that what you want? To confront Edric in battle?"

Rage kindled anew in Ash's veins. Confront wasn't a strong enough word to describe what he wanted to do to the bastard.

"He was your best friend!" she whispered.

"*Was.*"

Her gaze flickered, a subtle acknowledgement of his use of the past tense. "Whatever happened between you, Ash, I do not understand how you could hurt him in this way. Why kidnap me right before our wedding? Why would you—?"

Ash lowered his arms and slowly straightened. "As I said, I will tell you all, but not just yet."

Her eyes narrowed. "Ash—"

"Try and get some rest. When you are feeling better, we will talk again."

"*Rest?*" She snorted as if he'd suggested the impossible. "If you cannot, or *will* not, tell me why I am here, then I ask that you return me to Millenstowe Keep."

He laughed, a rough sound.

"Immediately," she added firmly.

He rose, the chair screeching back across the planks. His Briar Rose had grown thorns since he'd last seen her; hell, but he rather liked her angry and prickly. How he longed to kiss her, right here, right now. Instead, with the soft *creak* of leather, he clenched his hands into fists.

"If you return me to Millenstowe Keep," she said, as though choosing her words with care, "I am sure, once you have explained your reasons for what you did to my father and Edric, that—"

"You will remain here."

She gasped. "I do not want to stay here."

"Nevertheless, you will."

Her throat moved with a hard swallow. "You will

19

hold me prisoner?"

"If I must."

"In this solar? 'Tis your private chamber, is it not?"

"'Tis."

Her shortened breaths rasped between her lips. "I will *not* stay here. I will find a way to leave."

He didn't doubt she'd try, but this was his castle, and all of the folk within its walls were beholden to him. "Then, regrettably, I will do what I must to stop you."

"Regrettably?" Her voice sounded shrill. "Are you even capable of regret?"

The words struck like the lash of a whip. His anger flared, swift and scorching. "You have no idea what I am capable of."

She stared at him, her expression full of anger, yet also remorse. "What in God's name has happened to you, Ash?" she whispered. "What kind of man have you become?"

As Ash's expression darkened with fury, Rosetta tightened her grip on the bedding. The young lord she'd loved had changed so much. Years ago, she'd adored his lop-sided smile that caused a dimple to form in his right cheek; the mischief always twinkling in his eyes; his gentleness toward all folk and animals.

While she resented the arrogant way Ash had spoken to her, she also longed to know what circumstances had molded him into the toughened warrior he was now, because whatever had happened to him had been significant.

She'd heard that some knights who returned from Crusade never forgot the horrors of war. Ash had not only fought Saracens, but had been badly scarred, his features permanently altered. She couldn't imagine what that must be like, to be reminded every day, through one's own reflection, of battle, bloodshed, and lives lost.

"The kind of man I have become," Ash repeated, each word ground out like a piece of stone.

"You are not the lord I knew," she said.

"Nor should I be, after what I have experienced."

Her attention instinctively shifted to his scar. Words crowded up inside her, demanding to be released. Mayhap if she asked about his injury, she could reach him emotionally. If she could somehow revive their common bond, she could convince him to let her go.

She must try. If only she could think past her worsening headache—

"Your head," Ash said. "How does it feel now?"

Defiance stirred within her, urging her to insist that she was perfectly fine. Yet, he'd known her well enough years ago to be able to tell when she was lying—and he no doubt would still be able to tell. "'Tis pounding like a drum," she admitted.

"You have a nasty bump from your fall, as well as some bruises. There was no bleeding, though. The healer said—"

A knock sounded on the door.

Ash crossed to it and opened it.

The chestnut-haired young woman outside curtsied. "Milord, you have a visitor. He is waiting in the great hall."

"Thank you, Herta." Ash motioned for her to enter the solar, and she quickly brushed past him.

Rosetta met Ash's gaze once again. "You were speaking of the healer?"

"I will consult her and see what more we can do for your injuries," he said. "Meanwhile, if there is aught else that you need, just ask Herta."

"Well, since I may ask, I would like to move into another room. My staying in the lord's solar is rather..." Rosetta's face warmed. "Inappropriate."

"Milord," Herta said quickly, "I could—"

He raised his hand, halting her. "Milady, I am surprised you would complain. I have given you the finest bed in the keep."

"That is *not*—"

"I vow you are comfortable enough here in the solar."

Comfortable enough? Comfort was not at all the issue. She was betrothed to another man!

Glowering, Rosetta said, "May I ask for Herta to return me to Millenstowe Keep, then? I vow I would be most comfortable there, and my throbbing head would feel much better."

Ash chuckled, the barest hint of genuine mirth in his voice. "I had forgotten how stubborn you can be. The answer, though, is still nay."

Chapter Three

Seated in a chair facing the fire in the great hall, Ash turned the thin gold coin in his fingers. The artifact had been discovered at dawn that morning. When the missive with word of the find had reached Ash, he'd immediately understood the significance—and had vowed 'twas yet another good reason for him to stop Rosetta's wedding.

The gold gleamed in the fire glow. The image of a man's head, surrounded by ancient lettering, marked one side of the coin; a central flower shape and more lettering was on the other.

"I am glad you were able to get hold of it, Niles." Ash kept his voice hushed so the servants setting tables at the far end of the hall for the midday meal wouldn't hear.

The red-haired man sitting opposite him—a trusted local informant Ash had met through the King's men in London—grinned and sipped his mug of ale. "The bag of silver you gave me helped."

Ash nodded. He loathed bribes, but in this instance, he'd spared no expense to get hold of the coin and ensure that news of the find didn't spread throughout Warwickshire. Far too much was at risk, mayhap even the throne of

England. "If I remember correctly, you said a peasant dug it up in his back garden, along with his carrots?"

"Aye. Once he realized what he'd found, he tore up the rest of his vegetable plot, but did not find any more gold."

That makes at least two artifacts discovered in the local area over the years. Ash had never forgotten the ring Rosetta had found when he, she, and Edric had slipped away from Millenstowe Keep one scorching summer afternoon. He and Edric had both moved to Millenstowe within weeks of one another, and had served Rosetta's father first as pages, and then squires. When they'd been given the opportunity to move to a larger fortress closer to London, to train to become knights, he and Edric had decided to stay and receive their training at Millenstowe, because of their close friendship with Rosetta. She had been caring for her ill mother while being tutored in the ways of a lady of a castle—essential preparation for when she married.

That hot day, though, they'd all been eager to run away from their duties to enjoy a swim in the creek.

Breathing hard, Ash, Rosetta, and Edric paused in the field crowned by a circle of huge standing stones; according to old stories, the monument—like many others throughout England—had been built and left behind by ancient peoples. Farther across the field, water glimmered, part of the creek that ran through the windswept wheat that would soon be harvested.

"Come on," Ash said, eager to plunge into the cool, clear water. He wiped sweat from his brow and slid his other hand through Rosetta's. Her silk gown would slow her down in the wheat, but if they stayed on the footpath through the field, she'd still be able to run fast.

Edric launched into a sprint, clearly eager to be the first into the water. Impatience tugged at Ash, and he pulled Rosetta's arm, urging her to hurry.

She ran behind him, laughing, her gown rustling and her loose, golden hair floating behind her on the breeze.

Suddenly, she halted. "Wait!" Her hand slid free from his.

"Briar Rose!" Ash skidded to a halt and turned to face her.

"I saw something…" She peered down at the ground. By the hem of her gown, broken rocks pushed up through the dirt.

Ash set his hands on his hips. "Edric is going to get to the creek before us."

"Mmm." She crouched, her gown sweeping the dirt. Then, her face brightening, she pushed aside the leaves of a dandelion blooming beside a rock. "Got it!"

As she stood, gold glinted in her fingers.

"What is it?" He closed the distance between them and leaned in to press his forehead against hers. The wind blew strands of her hair across his face, and he swept them away as he gazed down at the treasure she'd found. "A ring," he murmured.

"While I was running, I saw a glint of light."

He gently cupped her hand in his. The gold band, slightly dented, had strange etchings on it, and was set with a dull red stone. A ruby? "That ring could have lain in the dirt for years before you found it."

"It does look like an old ring," she said, smiling.

"One that could have belonged to an ancient king or queen," Ash agreed.

"I must show Father when we get back to the keep."

Misgiving sifted through Ash. "Are you certain 'tis wise?"

"What do you mean? These are Father's lands—"

"I know, but if word gets out that there is treasure to be found, this whole field will be dug up within the week, as well as the surrounding lands. Folk will come from many leagues away to try to find a piece of gold."

"But—"

"And our creek, our special place, will be churned up into a pile of mud." He squeezed her hand. "None of us wants that, do we?" Selfish though it might be, he certainly didn't want to lose his favorite swimming spot for the rest of the summer.

Her worried blue eyes met his. "I do not want to lie to my father."

"You do not have to lie. You simply do not tell him."

"'Twill be our secret, you mean?"

"Aye."

Concern still lingered in her gaze. With his free hand, Ash tipped up her chin, bringing her lush pink mouth closer to his. He kissed her, their breaths mingling while their lips moved together in the perfect rhythm of give and take. With his mouth, he enticed and tempted. He relentlessly seduced, and with luck, he'd also convinced.

Finally, a satisfied groan rumbling in his throat, he released her. Eyelids closed, she stayed very still, as if caught up in the thrill of his kiss. Then, slowly, she opened her eyes. "Very well. Our secret."

"Oy!" Edric called from a distance. "What is keeping you two?"

Rosetta looked down at her gown, as if needing a place to stow the ring.

"I can keep it for you," Ash said, doing his best to hide his eagerness. "Until we get back to the keep."

She dropped the ring into his palm. He tucked it into the leather bag at his hip, caught her hand, and they raced together to join Edric…

"Milord."

Ash blinked and found himself still by the fire with Niles. "Does Lord Montgomery know of this find?"

"I cannot say, milord. What I *do* know is that the peasant tried to leave town to sell the gold—"

"Which is how you came to have it?"

Niles smiled, an unsettling twist of his mouth. "I never met the peasant. I came by the gold after negotiating with those who had acquired it through a particular…exchange."

A chill trailed through Ash, for he suspected the peasant had been murdered. A sad end for a poor man who had no doubt believed after finding the gold that his life had changed.

"Will those men with whom you negotiated keep silent about the coin?"

"I vow they will. They are businessmen, after all. Moreover, they have agreed to inform me straight away if they hear of any more gold being found." Niles wiped ale from his bottom lip. "I would not worry, milord. Even if the men do talk, the peasant was known to be a little addled in the head, thanks to his love of drink. Few people around here will believe that he really did find ancient gold amongst his vegetables. His story will become just another one of those tales that folk like to tell now and again."

"Good." Ash curled his hand around the coin. "You have done well to get this gold to me."

"'Tis why you—well, more accurately, the crown— pay me so well." Niles tipped his head back, finishing the last of his ale. Setting the empty mug down, he said, "Besides, you are the one man I trust to do what is right."

Ash frowned. "Right?"

"My gut instinct is never wrong. I know, with certainty, 'tis not the last we will hear of treasure to be found in these lands."

Caution hummed at the back of Ash's mind. He'd always believed there were more riches to be found on Lord Montgomery's lands than just the ring. Still, he mustn't agree too readily; 'twas clear he still had much to learn from Niles. "Why do you say that?"

"I have lived in Warwickshire for many years. I have heard the old stories of a vast hoard, lost riches of the Kingdom of Mercia, hidden somewhere close by. Some say 'tis enough Anglo-Saxon gold to fund a large army." Niles leaned forward, his eyes narrowing with purpose. "I believe, milord, that 'tis enough gold to enable supporters of John Lackland to overthrow our King. For that reason, I will gladly do all I can to keep the riches a secret."

Propped up in bed in the solar, the blankets tucked under her armpits, Rosetta fumed. How dare Ash treat her in such a manner? He had no right to be so bloody arrogant and unyielding. She wasn't a child, nor was she dim-witted. Edric would never have shown her such disrespect.

Her headache had become almost unbearable, and Rosetta struggled to ward off the unwelcome threat of tears. Herta had been summoned by the healer, so Rosetta was alone in the chamber.

'Twas the perfect moment to indulge in a good cry, but she would *not* be found weeping. The women in her family always endured, regardless of the ordeals they had to overcome. Rosetta's mother, after a difficult and heartbreaking stillbirth, had battled years of poor health, but through sheer strength of will, and her husband's unwavering love, she had fully recovered. Rosetta, too, would fight—and do her utmost to outwit Ash in any way possible.

Dear Edric. How was he faring? He and her parents must have been frantic with worry when they found her mare but not her. No doubt he'd sent his men-at-arms to question townsfolk and search every alley, shop, and home in Clipston, but of course, Rosetta wouldn't be found.

Her thoughts drifted to the last time she'd seen Edric—three days ago, when they'd walked down by the lake near Wallensford Keep.

Long grasses and wildflowers whispered against their garments as they wandered down to the still, glassy water. Edric had taken her hand from the moment they'd handed the reins of their horses to the men-at-arms who would stand guard nearby. He always held her hand whenever they were together now, as if he wanted to reinforce that she belonged to him—even though with the large pearl and emerald ring he'd given her on her left hand, there could be no mistaking that she was betrothed.

"You are quiet, my love," Edric murmured, brushing his thumb against hers. The callus on his thumb was rough against her skin.

"I am enjoying our lovely surroundings." She smiled at him. "When we are married, I hope we can bring picnics and spend quiet afternoons here."

"We can, my love. Whenever you like." His gaze smoldered and skimmed over her pale pink gown. "We can send the guards away and do far more than picnic, if we wish."

"Edric!"

He grinned, his expression reminding her of the lad he'd been when they had first met many years ago. "I cannot help being excited for our wedding. We will have a grand day, Rosetta, with the most talked-about festivities ever held in Warwickshire." His tone turned husky. "And that night in my bed, when I make you my wife in all ways—"

"I am sure 'twill all be wonderful," she said with a nervous giggle, not wanting to think about her wedding night. She'd always imagined that she would marry Ash and that he would be the man she lay with, but that obviously had been a fanciful dream.

Ash had returned to England a while ago and hadn't made any attempt to contact her. He also hadn't responded to any of her letters, which seemed strange. Ash also hadn't been invited to the wedding; Edric had said Ash would be away on estate business on the day of their nuptials and therefore an invitation hadn't been sent. The nagging disquiet inside her became a need to find out if her betrothed had any insights to share.

"Edric," she said as casually as possible. "Have you heard from Ash?"

"Ash?" He looked startled. "Nay. Why?"

"Did you not say that Ash would be away on the day we are to wed? How did you know that without speaking to him or receiving a missive from him?"

"I learned that bit of news while talking with a fellow lord."

"I see." Frowning, she said, "Do you not find it odd that Ash has not contacted us in any way?"

Edric shielded his eyes and watched the ducks gliding on the lake. "I am sure Ash is a very busy man now that he is lord of Damsley Keep."

"True, but surely he would want to—?"

"Have you heard from him?"

There was a curious edge to Edric's voice that somehow heightened her unease. "Regrettably, I have not," she said.

A smile touched Edric's lips.

"It just seems strange that Ash has chosen to—"

Sighing, Edric freed his hand from hers and then slid his arm around her waist while they walked. "Why are we talking about Ash? We are marrying in a few days. I want to talk about us, the places we want to visit, how many children we hope to have—"

A knock sounded on the solar door, bringing Rosetta back to the present. Herta peered in, and her face brightened with a smile. "Oh, good, you are still awake. I have a drink for you, specially made by the healer to ease your headache."

The young woman crossed to the bed, and Rosetta reluctantly accepted the earthenware mug. She'd learned a fair bit about healing infusions during her mother's illness. The local healer had created concoctions of various blends of herbs, including powerful ones made from Poppy and Valerian for when her mother was suffering pain. Would Ash have asked his healer to use such sleep-inducing herbs? 'Twould be an easy way to keep Rosetta from trying to escape.

Her hand tightened around the warm mug. She *was* going to get away.

"Drink, milady," Herta urged in that sweet way of hers.

"What is in this infusion?"

"Herbs. Honey. Sometimes the healer also adds

spices."

Rosetta breathed in the sweetish, earthy scent of the drink.

Herta sat in the chair beside the bed, her hands clasped on her lap. "'Tis not going to harm you."

Rosetta laughed, the sound brittle. "Are you certain?"

"Of course! Milord is a kind, gallant man who would never harm a woman. Not deliberately."

"Not deliberately? Do you mean he has hurt women before?"

"Oh, nay, not at all." A blush stained Herta's cheeks. "Lord Blakeley made sure that after one of the maidservants burned her hands in the kitchens—she accidentally knocked over a pan of hot chicken fat—she did not return to her duties for a week. A whole week! I know of no other lord who has shown such compassion toward a commoner. He has also ordered that everyone within this castle has a full meal every day. No one is to go hungry."

Ash had certainly won Herta's adoration, and likely that of every other servant at Damsley Keep. With effort, Rosetta swallowed her indignant reply that he had hurt her by kidnapping her.

"The drink will help you feel better," Herta continued, her gaze earnest. "Surely you do not intend to spend all of your stay here abed?"

Most certainly not—especially when, through no choice of her own, she was occupying Ash's bed. Yet, as much as she wanted to flee, Rosetta had to admit she wasn't up to the challenge right now. After a rest, when her headache was gone, though…

She brought the mug to her lips and sipped. The drink tasted of honey and mint, but had a slightly bitter aftertaste. She drank it all down.

"Well done, milady." Herta took back the mug. "Now, is there aught else you would like? Shall I order you some fare?"

"Not just now," Rosetta said. "Are my garments and shoes clean yet? I would like them back."

"I will ask," Herta said, rising. She hurried to the door and spoke with someone outside: A guard? Knowing Ash, he would have posted more than one in the corridor.

Rosetta leaned back against her pillows. Already she was feeling drowsy. Mayhap she shouldn't have downed the drink so quickly. She trapped a yawn with her hand and fought to stay awake, but her heavy eyelids slipped closed.

"Is she all right?" Ash asked from the doorway, his gaze on Rosetta.

"Aye, milord," Herta whispered from the chair by the bed. "Just asleep."

He walked to the bed, as quietly as possible. Twilight had fallen, and after confirming that extra guards were patrolling the battlements and on duty at the gatehouse, he'd no longer been able to resist seeing Rosetta again.

Standing at the bedside, he studied her sleeping face. How lovely she was, lying on her back with her shimmering golden hair flowing over the pillow. Her skin was smooth and dewy, and her thick lashes brushed her cheeks. She looked peaceful and exquisitely beautiful, but once she woke, he would face her flashing eyes and biting words once more.

His gloved hand lifted, gently smoothed back a stray wisp of hair so that it blended into the rest of her tresses by her right temple. How he wanted to trail his bare fingers down the slope of her cheek and wake her, as he once had in the meadow near Millenstowe Keep, with a tender kiss. Years ago, she'd sighed blissfully, her eyelids had fluttered open, and he'd felt the loving warmth of her gaze the instant their eyes had met; he'd cherished her and the wonder of belonging to her.

She wouldn't look at him that way now. In time, mayhap, but not now.

His hand curled, the black leather of his glove tightening across his knuckles. He eased away from the bed, the familiar rage and bitterness filling his soul. Truth be told, she might never love him again, for he was damaged, even repugnant.

"Milord?" Herta asked softly, sounding concerned.

"When she wakes, summon me."

Ash quit the solar, nodding to the two guards outside as he left, and headed down the passageway to the arched door that opened onto the narrow stone steps up to the battlements. As he shut the iron-banded door at the top of the stairs, the wind tugged at his garments and brought the scent of old, sun-warmed stone.

He strode to the edge of the battlement to look down into the bailey, where servants were lighting the torches that would burn through the night. All that he could see around him was his; all that he could not see within the fortress was his too, including Rosetta. He'd made her a promise years ago, that she would always be his. She might not care to remember, but he did. Ash never broke a promise.

The battlement door banged open behind him. He reached on instinct for the knife at his belt, but his hand fell away when he saw who approached.

"Good evening, Uncle."

"Good evening, Justin." As the six-year-old boy reached his side, Ash ruffled his shaggy mop of dark blond hair. "How are the pups tonight?"

Justin's brown eyes shone. Judging by the straw clinging to his tunic, the lad had just come from the stable, where the wolfhound had birthed her litter a few weeks ago in an empty stall. "They all have fat little bellies and seem to be well."

"'Tis good news."

"Can I have one of the puppies? Please?"

Ash chuckled.

"Please?"

"Well…" Ash scratched his chin. While he had already decided to let Justin have his pick of the litter—the healer had suggested the pet might help to comfort the boy and ease his nightmares—Ash would prefer that Justin earn the reward. Working toward a goal would be good for the lad. 'Twould help him gain fighting skills that he would need to become a knight one day, and would also help him focus on matters other than his father's recent death. Ash was now the boy's guardian, since Justin's mother had died eighteen months ago in childbirth.

"I will practice with my bow," the lad said.

Ash's brows rose. His late brother had been a highly skilled archer. While Ash had had a bow specially made for Justin, the boy had yet to use it very often. "Will you now?"

Justin nodded in earnest.

"Very well. If you can hit the largest archery target by the time the pups are weaned, you may keep one."

Jumping up and down, Justin grinned. "I cannot decide whether I want the smallest one or the one with the shaggiest tail."

"You have plenty of time to decide. The pups are not old enough to leave their mother yet."

"True." Justin's smile wobbled, and then he threw himself at Ash and wrapped his arms around him, pressing his cheek against Ash's stomach. "Thank you, Uncle."

Ash closed his arms around the boy's thin shoulders. He stood quietly, silently sharing the lad's happiness and also grief. Losing a brother to a corrupted wound was difficult; losing a beloved father was even more so.

After long moments, Justin drew away. He quickly wiped his eyes on his grubby sleeve, no doubt hoping Ash wouldn't notice. With a pang of remorse, Ash made a mental note to buy the lad some new clothes when he had the chance. Justin's tunic was stained, too short in the sleeves, and ripped at the hem, and the rest of his garments were in equally bad condition, despite the servants' best efforts to care for them.

"I am going to go inside now," the boy said. "The wind is growing cold."

"All right." Night was settling in, falling like darkening ink across the castle and surrounding lands.

"Uncle…"

"Aye?" Ash murmured.

"Will you have time for a game of chess tonight?"

Ash smiled, for the boy was just like his father in his love of such games. "Regrettably, we must postpone our game for tonight." As the lad's face crumpled with disappointment, Ash added, "There is a lady—a special guest—staying in my chamber. I do not wish to disturb her by fetching the chess set."

"Tomorrow, then?"

"Aye. Tomorrow."

"Some wine, milady?"

"Thank you." Pushing herself up to sitting, Rosetta accepted the goblet from Herta. The woman had told her 'twas dark outside now, which meant Rosetta had slept most of the afternoon, no doubt due to the herbal drink.

Truth be told, though, she did feel much better, although her brow still ached a bit, and her mind was fuzzy, as though she were trying to think with a head full of newly-shorn wool.

"Did you ask about my garments and shoes?" Rosetta asked.

"I am sorry, milady, but they are still being cleaned, along with your veil. The maidservants are having trouble getting out the mud stains. One of the women gave me this, though." She collected a folded item from the trestle table and brought it to the bed.

The garment was a forest green gown made of coarse linen. Not at all what a lady would wear, but at least Rosetta would have more to wear than a chemise. Shoes, though, were essential if she was going to flee the keep. She'd have to find a pair as soon as possible.

"Shall we see how the gown fits, milady?" Herta asked, shaking out the garment.

Rosetta placed the goblet on the bedside table. "All right."

She managed to pull aside the bedding and step down onto the floorboards, although her head swam. She quickly sat on the side of the bed and drew in deep breaths. Once her head had stopped reeling, she stood and pulled on the gown.

Herta fastened the ties down the sides. "Once you are dressed, you can see his lordship."

See Ash again? She'd rather eat a bucketful of pickled frogs. "Nay, Herta—"

"He has invited you to join him in the great hall. He said you would likely be hungry after your rest."

A shudder trailed through Rosetta, but she swiftly rallied her anger. Smoothing her long hair with her fingers, she said, "I have no wish to see him again. *Ever.*"

Herta made a small sound of distress and then went to the doorway, as if to relay Rosetta's words.

Turning her back to the door, Rosetta hugged herself

and walked to the fire, its flames casting an inviting warmth across the patterned rug. She'd already determined there was little she could use as a weapon in the chamber. Ash had obviously figured out her first thoughts would be to escape.

Mayhap she'd find something of use in Ash's linen chests? Without a weapon, she couldn't get past the guards outside. She glanced at the wooden chests, but they both bore iron locks. Unless she found the keys, she'd have to find a way to smash the chests open.

Hushed voices carried in the corridor, and then the door clicked shut.

"Thank you for telling his lordship that I—"

"—never wished to see him again?" Rough laughter reached her, and the fine hairs on her nape prickled. She looked back to find Ash leaning against the door, arms crossed over his chest. "Bold words, Briar Rose, but they will not keep me from seeing *you* whenever I wish."

Chapter Four

"What do you want, Ash?" Rosetta demanded.

You. He smothered the impulse to voice that desire, and said instead, "Since you will not dine with me in the great hall, I am bringing the meal to you."

"I am not hungry."

He grinned, a roguish curve of his mouth. "Oh, but I am." He let his gaze wander to her lips and then down the elegant column of her throat to her bosom, as if she stood naked before him and he was appreciating what he saw—which he was. The bliaut wasn't her usual style or quality of garment, but she still looked lovely.

Her gaze sharpened with annoyance, and she crossed her arms, mimicking his posture. From her expression, she was clearly struggling with the urge to walk over and slap him. That, however, would mean getting close to him, and he sensed her reluctance to draw near.

Was she afraid of him, or her own feelings for him? She must know that he'd never physically harm her, not under any circumstances, so that meant she didn't trust herself. How intriguing.

A muffled clattering nose came from outside. Easing

away from the door, Ash opened it, and servants entered, carrying a folding oak table.

"By the hearth," he said.

Rosetta moved back as they set up the table. More servants followed with a linen cloth, wine, goblets, a platter of sliced bread, and bowls of stew. After pushing two chairs up to the table, the servants left, leaving him and Rosetta alone in the solar.

She hadn't moved from her spot near his linen chests.

"Come," he said, gesturing to the table.

"As I said—"

"I know what you said. I also know that you have not eaten since you arrived."

"You care so much about my eating habits?"

I care so much about you. "I am responsible for everyone within my castle, including my guests." He crossed to the table and sat. "The cook makes a good rabbit stew. 'Tis best eaten warm, not cold."

She remained where she was, her fingers drumming on her arms. Picking up a spoon, he dipped it into the rich brown broth, scooped up chunks of parsnip and carrot, and then ate the mouthful. He'd already eaten a while ago in the great hall with the rest of his subjects, but she didn't need to know that. "Delicious," he said.

"Ash—"

There was a plea in her voice that hadn't been there before. Good. If he persisted, she would likely yield. He sure as hell wasn't going to give in.

"At least try the stew," he said, bestowing on her his most charming smile. "Please?"

She sighed. Her arms fell to her sides, and she walked to the vacant chair and sat.

"Thank you."

"If you are here, Ash, because you want me to eat—"

"I am."

"I will. Then you will have no reason to stay."

God's bones, but she was stunning, her eyes glittering with resolve and her cheekbones darkened with a rosy flush. A mischievous part of him wanted to goad her more, but she had agreed to sit and eat. He'd rather not ruin his small victories thus far.

"Once I have eaten, I will leave," he agreed and poured her some wine. "In the meanwhile, I was hoping we could talk."

She spooned up some stew and eyed him warily. "Talk?"

"We have not spoken to one another in years. There is much for us to catch up on."

"I did not think you were at all interested in getting reacquainted."

His brows rose. "Why do you say that?"

"As I mentioned before, you did not answer my letters. Nor have you made any effort to contact me—or Edric—in any other manner, even though you returned to England some time ago."

Ash clenched his jaw. "There were good reasons for—"

"So, if you intend to ask about my relationship with Edric, beware. I do not believe I owe you any explanations."

Oh, he did want to know about Edric, but Ash doubted she would speak of such personal matters until he had regained a little more of her trust. Sipping his wine, he waited for her to finish her mouthful. "To be honest, I would rather not discuss Edric right now. Let us begin with something easy. How are your parents?"

"Fine."

"Still living at Millenstowe Keep, I understand."

"Aye."

"Your older sister?"

"She married three summers ago. She and her lord husband live in Derbyshire and have two children, a son and a daughter."

He fought not to smile as Rosetta took another spoonful of stew, her expression softening with delight in what she was tasting.

"What about your parents?" she asked. "I remember meeting them years ago, when they came to visit you at Millenstowe."

Regret lanced through him. "Both dead."

Shock widened her eyes. "Oh, Ash. I am sorry."

"So am I. They died while I was away on Crusade. They caught the sickness sweeping through my father's lands and…never recovered."

She looked down at her stew. "Truly, I am sorry. I cannot imagine losing one parent, let alone both of them."

He drank more wine, wishing he could ease the pain of losing his family. "My brother inherited my sire's keep. He ruled it until he perished from a leg injury that festered and spread corruption through his body. He died about a month ago, soon after I had returned to England. His son inherited, but he is very young and upset at losing both of his parents; his mother, you see, died a while ago in childbirth. I arranged with the crown to have the keep managed in his stead until he is old enough, and ready, to rule."

"I see." She took a piece of the wheat bread and broke off a chunk. "Thanks to the King, you also have a castle of your own now."

"Damsley is a fine fortress."

"Your estate also borders my father's lands," she said, her gaze holding his, "just like Edric's."

Ah. So she did know what a tremendous prize she was as a bride.

"You are no doubt aware that Edric's father died not long ago," she continued, dipping her bread into her stew, "so he became lord of Wallensford Keep."

Caution sifted through Ash. He remembered hearing about the older Lord Sherborne's demise from an informant, who had been convinced the death hadn't been natural; no proof of murder, though, had been found. "I had heard that Edric's sire died, but—"

"Is that why you abducted me before I could be married? Because you do not want Edric to lay claim to my father's lands when my sire dies?"

Ash glanced at the fire, his mouth pressing into a hard line. He couldn't deny the prospect of expanding his estate was an enticing one. However, there was far more at stake than his own personal gain.

"You have gone quiet," she mused.

"I am deciding how to respond," he countered.

"You could just be honest and admit I was right."

His gloved hand tightened on the stem of his goblet. "I could. However—"

"You would rather not confirm the truth."

He hissed a breath through his teeth. There was so much he wanted to tell her, but couldn't. To ensure her safety, he had to keep his secrets, especially when much of his investigation was still ongoing. "I will not confirm what others, who do not know all of the facts, may well misinterpret."

Surprise lit her features. "Misinterpret? Every lord wants more wealth and lands. From childhood, he is brought up to strive for those things."

"True. Not every nobleman is willing to do what others are, though, in order to get those riches and lands."

Her spoon landed in her bowl with a metallic *clink*. "Are you saying—?"

"Mmm?"

Her eyes sparked with fury. "Are you implying Edric's only reason for marrying me is to eventually gain more riches and lands?"

Ash downed more wine, delaying his answer. The drink left a bitter taste in his mouth.

"Edric *cares* for me."

Nowhere near as much as I care about you.

"He respects me."

As do I, Briar Rose.

"He has been my closest friend through the years, especially after his return from the East, and…and you have *no* right to make such an outlandish claim."

Anger coiled through Ash, rising up from the simmering resentment that had been sown the day he'd been attacked. The blood streaming down into his eyes and running from his hands had been naught compared to the agony of betrayal. "You are mistaken," he bit out. "I have every right."

Rosetta's heart pounded in her breast. Ash looked so forbidding, she wanted to shrink back in the chair. Yet, she mustn't show weakness. She'd learned more about Ash in the past few moments than she had in all the years he'd been away, and if she wanted to outwit him, she needed to understand his reasons for acting and speaking as he had.

"Why do you believe you have such a right?"

His gaze narrowed until his eyes were glinting slits. "I know Edric better than anyone."

"Because you are best friends?" At the last moment, she remembered he'd spoken of the friendship in the past tense.

"*Were* best friends." Ash's fingers tightened again on his wine goblet, and as the leather pulled taut across his hand, he grimaced. Ash couldn't be comfortable wearing his gloves indoors, and yet, she hadn't seen him without them. Why? Had he injured his hands?

As he relaxed his grip on the vessel and the discomfort faded from his features, past memories tugged at her: Ash and Edric laughing and throwing buckets of water at one another in the bailey of Millenstowe Keep; the two of them with arms draped around each other's shoulders, grinning after winning prizes at the local tournament; Ash and Edric riding side by side over the drawbridge as they began their journey to join the King's army and travel to far off lands to battle the Saracens, with no guarantee that they would ever return to Warwickshire.

"You were close friends with Edric when you left for Crusade."

The barest hint of regret flickered in Ash's burning eyes. "Indeed, we were inseparable for many months while we sailed, marched, and battled for our King. We made other friends too, with lords who had traveled from all over England to go on Crusade. Many of them…" His bronzed throat moved with a swallow, and he looked back at the fire, his expression shadowed by grief. "They did not survive."

"That must have been very difficult for you," she murmured. She set aside the bread; it had started to taste like straw.

"Difficult is a far from adequate word." He dragged a gloved hand over his chin and jaw. "One of the reasons I returned to Warwickshire months later than Edric was that I wanted to honor some of our friends' dying wishes. One of the lords from London asked that I give his betrothed his signet ring so she'd always remember him. I needed the crown's help to find out where she lived. There were others…" His words trailed off to silence, filled only by the snap and pop of the fire.

He suddenly seemed lonely, his soul heavy with the

weight of his memories. Rosetta longed to reach across the table and touch his hand, but there was no point; he'd never feel the heat of her skin through the leather.

"I also left the East later than Edric did because I needed to heal," Ash said quietly. "I was badly wounded when the Knights Hospitaller took me into their care. They spent long days and nights treating my injuries, but feared the wounds would become corrupted, and I would die. My fellow soldiers, you see, did not find me for some time after I was attacked, because I had become separated from the rest of the army."

Rosetta feared for him even as she knew he had lived to tell his tale. "Did you not call for help?"

"I shouted until I was hoarse, while I prayed over and over that I would be found by friends and not the Saracens. I damaged my throat. My voice has never fully recovered." His shoulders lifted in a stiff shrug. "The Knights Hospitaller also feared I might lose all use of my hands, but thanks to their efforts, that did not happen."

"Mother Mary!" She couldn't keep the horror from her voice.

His fiery gaze locked with hers. "You must have noticed my gloves."

"A-aye, but—"

"I wear them to spare others from seeing just how repugnant my hands are now."

The barely leashed rage in his voice sapped the breath from her lungs.

"My caregivers did what they could to help me. They used different kinds of poultices, ointments, and some other treatments I barely remember because…"

"Because?"

"I was in pain, and I was angry." He scowled. "I did not want to be lying in a hospital bed. I wanted revenge, but they insisted that my life depended upon me resting and focusing on my healing. When I received a missive from King Richard, ordering me to stay with the Knights Hospitaller, I had to obey."

As though speaking of his hands had made him self-conscious, he linked them together atop the table, the leather of his gloves whispering.

"The scar across your brow is not so awful," she managed to say. "Neither, I am sure, are the scars on your hands."

He laughed roughly. "They are more than enough to make a gently-raised maiden swoon."

Did he mean that they would make *her* swoon? She frowned, for she hated that he would assume such a thing. "Should I not be able to make that judgment for myself?"

Ash shook his head. "No one sees my hands. *No one.*"

Her heart ached for him. What must it be like not to be able to touch another person? To be denied the sensations of warmth or softness beneath one's fingertips? To be forbidden the pleasure of giving…a caress?

Years ago, he had touched her as though he loved the feel of her skin, as though she was precious and treasured—

She forced aside the unwelcome thoughts.

"What are you thinking?" Ash asked softly.

She reached for her goblet of wine. "If you must know, I am honored that you shared—"

"Nay, you are not." The corner of his mouth ticked up. "You might not care to remember that I once knew you *intimately*—"

She gasped. She had *not* lain with him, although she'd wanted to, so very much.

"—but I have not forgotten."

Rosetta bit down on her bottom lip and struggled to keep hold of her emotions. She didn't want to talk about their past together, although he seemed to be luring her down that hazardous path. He must realize they could never go back to those days now that she was bound by her betrothal to Edric—no matter how wondrous their relationship had been, or how much he'd once meant to her.

"I *know* what you are thinking," Ash said, his tone a gritty rasp. "You wish I had never returned to England."

"Ash—"

"You cannot stand to look upon me with my ugly scars—"

"Not true!"

"—and you *hate* that I prevented Edric from taking you to his bed—"

Her hand moved, purely on instinct. She hurled the rest of her wine at him. The ruby red liquid splashed his face and dripped down onto the front of his tunic.

Before she could fully register what she'd done, he'd risen from his chair and was upon her. His gloved hands closed on her arms, hauling her to her feet.

"Ash! Stop," she screeched, struggling. She clawed at his tunic, tried to break his imprisoning hold, but he was so much faster, bigger, and stronger. He propelled her backward, his muscled legs knocking hers, his breath as hot as fire on her brow. Her heels hit the wall and she gasped, breathless, as he pinned her against the cold, rough stone.

Fear tingled through her, but also a wild, wicked excitement.

He growled like a wounded beast and set his right hand to her throat. Cool leather pressed against Rosetta's skin, causing a shiver to ripple down her spine. His hand shook, but gently, so gently, he forced her chin up with his thumb.

She tried to avoid meeting his gaze, how she tried, but the heat of his stare bored into her until she had no choice but to look at him. What she saw in his eyes made her tremble. "Ash," she whispered.

"Aye, *Ash*," he answered, his voice hitching on what sounded like a sob. "Not Edric. *Ash*."

Before she could say a word, Ash lowered his head and kissed her.

Chapter Five

Rosetta tasted of heartfelt promises, forgotten dreams, and a true love Ash never wanted to relinquish. Shuddering, he crushed his lips to hers. Her sweet fragrance mingled with the piquant scent of the wine soaking into his tunic, and his mind revived every nuance of every kiss they'd ever shared.

Her mouth tasted wondrous. Her slender body, crushed against his, fitted perfectly, just as he'd remembered. Just as he'd dreamed, while he'd slept on the ground at Acre. Just as he'd desired.

He longed to lose himself in the intoxicating pleasure of her kiss, as he'd done years ago. Rosetta, though, remained very still. Her whole body was rigid while his lips moved over hers. Her mouth stayed shut. Unyielding.

His lips glided, pressed, *demanded* that she respond by kissing him back. As she remained unresponsive, a groan of frustration welled within him. Had she forsaken him? She couldn't love Edric, the cold-hearted bastard. God's blood, but she couldn't.

He squeezed his eyes shut, fought the sting of bitter tears, as he kissed her.

Still, she didn't kiss him back.

The rage within him softened under the burn of regret. A tear slipped from Ash's eyes and ran down his cheek. He'd loved her every day that he'd been away from her, and he loved her still. He'd rather die than have her marry another lord, especially Edric. Yet, how did he show her what she meant to him? He couldn't lose her again. He *couldn't.*

Despair gripped Ash, just as a betraying tremor raced through her. Hope sparked within him, the smallest ember of encouragement, and he gentled his kiss. With his lips, the sweep of his tongue, he asked her to remember him the way he was years ago. He coaxed, teased, and tempted, focusing all of his love for her into his kiss.

A moan broke from her.

"Briar Rose," he whispered against her mouth. So tenderly, he kissed her. Fighting the need to deepen the kiss, to take control, he lowered his hand from her throat and slid it into her silken hair. How he wished he could feel her tresses brushing against his fingers, but he mustn't be greedy; at least he was touching her.

Rosetta sighed, her breath warm against his lips.

She shivered, and then she kissed him back.

Relief rushed through him, followed by an overwhelming surge of joy. Their mouths meshed, slowly at first, and with utmost tenderness. Then, as she initiated a deeper kiss, his pent-up emotions could no longer be contained. His kisses quickened, deepened. His breaths became impassioned rasps. His hands slid down to settle at her waist; hers buried into the front of his tunic. Ah, God, he wanted to drown in the fury of the desire she was unleashing, to kiss her and kiss her until they were both gasping and straining for—

A rap sounded on the solar door.

Breaking the kiss, he cursed softly.

Rosetta, her eyes glazed with need, blinked up at him.

Her lips were red and swollen from his kisses.

Another knock, and the solar door creaked inward. "Milord?" Herta called.

Rosetta dashed sideways along the wall. He spun away, wiping his face with his sleeve. As Herta stepped inside, he noted that Rosetta had reached the hearth and stood facing it, her arms crossed, her back to him and the maidservant.

"I am sorry, milord," Herta said, "but you asked me—"

Ash nodded. He had indeed asked her to fetch him if Justin needed him. "I will be there in a moment." Herta smiled and began to retreat, and Ash added, "We have finished dining. Send servants to clear away the table."

"Right away, milord."

When the young woman had left, he crossed to the hearth, but Rosetta's shoulders stiffened. The intimacy they'd shared moments ago was gone, as if it had never happened.

But it had, and he'd be damned if he would let it go.

Beside her now, he set his hand in the small of her back. Her chin nudged higher, causing the glossy fall of her hair to brush against his arm. "After that kiss—" he murmured.

"Please leave, Ash," she said quietly.

"I must, for the moment, but—"

"Just *go!*"

The desperation in her voice both encouraged and scorned him. How he longed to take her in his arms again, to kiss her one last time before he left.

Instead, his hand fell away from her, and he turned on his heel and walked out.

Rosetta remained by the hearth while the servants carried out the table and what remained of the meal. Once they had left, though, she crumpled into a heap on the glazed hearth tiles. Pressing her hand to her mouth to smother the sound, she wept.

She should have resisted Ash. She should have found the strength within her to shove him away and rail at him for daring to try and kiss her. Her marriage to Edric had been sanctioned by the crown, and 'twas nigh impossible to break such a commitment. And yet, while in Ash's arms, even as those thoughts had clamored within her, her foolish heart had embraced the chance to kiss him once more. He was the only man she had ever loved, and her heart hadn't forgotten.

Oh, mercy, what had she *done*? How would she explain her moment of weakness to Edric? Honorable, handsome, loyal Edric, who cared for her so much that he had asked her to be his wife. He hadn't given up on her when she'd turned him down the first two times he had proposed, which surely proved he really did love her.

Tears streamed down her cheeks and dripped onto her gown. Sniffling, she gathered her tattered emotions. She couldn't change what had happened, but she could prevent it from occurring again.

After pushing to her feet, she wiped her eyes and then strode to the bedside table. When Herta had brushed out Rosetta's hair, she'd removed all of the pins that had held the braid in place and left them in a neat pile. Rosetta picked up a pin and headed to Ash's linen chests.

She knelt on the planks beside the smaller of the two chests. Lifting the iron lock, she shoved the pin into the opening.

Metal scraped against metal, but the lock didn't click.

She pulled out the pin and tried again. She pushed, twisted, and shoved.

The lock didn't budge.

Frustration bubbled inside her. There had to be a way to get into the chest. Mayhap the pin wasn't thick enough to trigger the internal workings of the lock?

She retrieved another pin. Using both of them at the same time, she pushed and wiggled them into the lock. *Work*, she silently begged. *Please.*

With a gritty *click*, the lock sprang open.

Muffled sobs reached Ash as he entered Justin's chamber. Regret gnawed at Ash for his brief but necessary delay; he had changed out of his wine-soaked tunic and shirt, to avoid the questions the ever-curious boy would undoubtedly ask if he saw the soaked garments.

Several candles burned beside the bed, their glow piercing through enough shadow that Ash could see the boy lying on his side beneath the blankets. Justin was facing the wall, his hair an unruly tangle on the pillow.

As Ash approached, the sheets rustled. Justin wiped at his face and then rolled over, his face blotchy from crying.

"Another bad dream?"

Justin nodded. "I…I dreamed about Father."

Ash knelt beside the bed and stroked mussed hair away from the boy's forehead. "I am sorry."

"I…I miss him."

"I know," Ash murmured, as the boy began to sob again, his cries racking his small body.

Ash rose and sat on the edge of the bed, the stone wall against his back. He pulled Justin up to lean against him and then tucked the blankets around the child to keep away the night chill. With his arm around the boy, Ash listened to the lad weep; Ash offered his handkerchief, comforting words, and hugs whenever he sensed they were needed.

How he hoped that what he was doing was of some help to Justin, for he had no experience at being a father or a guardian. Ash hadn't been involved much in Justin's life until a few weeks ago, and he certainly didn't want to fail in the responsibility he'd brought upon himself so that the boy would be raised by a relative and not a stranger.

One thing Ash did understand that he and Justin shared: anguish. It ate at one's soul, day and night. It robbed one of sleep and taunted in moments of self-doubt. At least, though, Justin didn't have physical wounds to overcome. For that, Ash was grateful.

At last, Justin's sobs diminished and then quieted. Ash remained still, waiting for the boy to tell him that he was ready to try and go back to sleep.

Justin rubbed at his eyes and then gazed up at Ash.

"Feeling any better?" Ash gently asked.

"A little."

"Good."

Justin blew his nose on the rather soggy handkerchief. "I was wondering…"

"Mmm?" Ash fought an encroaching yawn.

"Will you stay in my room tonight? If I have another nightmare—"

"Of course I will stay. I will ask servants to bring a cot and bedding in here for me. It might get a bit cramped in your room—"

"I do not mind," Justin said.

Ash smiled. "Neither do I. I have a few matters to attend, but when I am ready to sleep, I will come straight here."

The boy was quiet a long while. Ash almost believed the child to be asleep, when he said, "Did you see the lady tonight? The one you did not want to disturb to get the chess set?"

Ash managed to keep the surprise from his voice. "Aye, I saw her." *And I kissed her.*

"What is she like?"

"She is golden-haired, strong of will, clever…"

"What color are her eyes?"

"Blue." Without doubt, they were the prettiest eyes Ash had ever seen.

"Is she tall?"

Ash remembered the feel of her crushed against him. "Not too tall." Indeed, her height was just perfect for kissing her.

"And beautiful?" Justin peered up at Ash.

Heat spread across Ash's face as he studied the lad. "Why do you ask?" Narrowing his eyes, he said, "Do you intend to woo her?"

Justin giggled. "Uncle! Do not be silly."

Ash grinned; 'twas good to hear the boy laugh.

"I merely wanted to be certain she was beautiful," the lad said, his words sounding a little drowsy. "Ladies always are, are they not? They are in the old stories you have told me at bedtime, those ones about fearless knights who have to fight bad men to rescue the damsels they love."

A wry chuckle tickled Ash's damaged throat. Justin had listened more closely to those tales of romance and adventure than Ash had thought.

"She is indeed very beautiful," he murmured. *And she is mine.*

Rosetta lifted the lid of the linen chest, and the scents of wood, leather, and clean garments rose up to her. Lying atop the folded clothes were four pairs of gloves, all black, as well as several sheathed daggers.

She removed the gloves and weapons, a chill chasing through her at the feel of the supple leather against her fingers. Her skin across her chin and throat still felt cool from where Ash's gloved hand had held her, while the rest of her body burned. How shameful that his kiss had ignited such sinful heat within her, cravings she had last experienced with him in the days before he'd left for Crusade. 'Twas surely wrong for her to desire one man but to be betrothed to another.

Leaning over the open chest, she removed some of the garments. Only three of the items of clothing bore embroidery. The rest were plain—unusual for the wardrobe of a nobleman, especially one who had been granted an estate by the crown. 'Twould seem that in most instances, Ash wanted to keep his noble rank a secret.

How curious.

At the bottom of the chest, she found a sheathed eating dagger, a box containing quills and ink, and a leather bag filled with pieces of silver. There was also a collection of rolled documents bound with twine.

She carefully untied the bundle. Several parchments bound together at the top left corner held a list of lord's names along with dates and locations, among them, local taverns, a mill on the outskirts of Clipston, and a tanner's premises. Edric's name was on the list, but her father's was not.

Three other missives… Her breath caught as she recognized the parchment supplied to Millenstowe Keep by a local merchant. As she unfurled the cured skin, she recognized her own penmanship. Ash had kept her letters, even though he had not answered them. Yet, the fact that he'd kept them caused a knot to settle in her stomach, for he wouldn't have kept them if he hadn't cared. Why, though, hadn't he replied?

Unable to ward off a growing sense of unease, she

unfurled the last parchment. "Mother Mary!" she whispered as her gaze skimmed the black ink drawing. 'Twas crudely done, but there was no mistaking the image of the gold ring she'd discovered on her father's lands, along with notes on the jewel's size, where it had been found, and the decoration etched into the gold band.

The day she'd found the ring, she had given it to Ash for safekeeping. He had said he would give it back to her when they returned to the keep, but the moment they'd walked through the gates, Ash and Edric had been sent to answer to the captain of the guard for disappearing when they'd had chores to complete. Ash and Edric had been absent from the evening meal, and she hadn't seen either of them again until the following morning, when Ash had passed her in a stairwell and pressed the ring into her hand.

She had stowed the jewel in her chamber, behind a loose stone to the left of the hearth. When last she had checked, 'twas still there. That meant Ash must have done the drawing years ago, most likely the night of the find.

Why had he made the sketch? What reason did he have for wanting to keep a record of the jewel? He'd been so insistent that they keep the ring a secret from her sire.

Only Ash could answer her questions, but asking him outright would be unwise. What she'd found were only fragments of what seemed to be a much greater puzzle. If she confronted him now, she might never learn what was really going on.

Her hands shook as she gathered the parchments and retied them the way she'd found them. Just as she started placing the garments back into the chest, voices sounded outside the solar door.

Rosetta quickly returned the items to the chest. As she started to close the lid, she hesitated, opened it again, and retrieved the eating dagger. Ash wouldn't miss it—not like the daggers he had stowed within easy reach atop his clothes.

She fastened the lock. Just as she kicked the knife and hairpins under the edge of the patterned rug, the door opened.

"Milady." Looking flustered, Herta walked in with a large earthenware pitcher. Her eyes widening, she abruptly halted. "Oh, goodness, I think I forgot to knock. Please forgive me, Lady Montgomery. Several maidservants went to bed early complaining of upset stomachs, so there are fewer of us to do all of the evening tasks. Now, the healer is making another herbal drink for you, and 'twill arrive shortly. I have heated water here for your nightly wash. Shall I help you untie your gown so you can bathe?"

Chapter Six

S wallowing a warm mouthful of cooked oats and milk, Ash looked out across the great hall illuminated by early morning sunshine streaming in through the hall's high, horn-covered windows. A sense of pride filled him at the sight of the men, women, and children gathered at the trestle tables to break their fast. Damsley Keep was a fine fortress, a place he was proud to call his home. If all went as he hoped over the coming days, Rosetta would soon be dining at his side as his wife, the servants equally beholden to her as well as to him.

Seated beside Ash at the imposing, carved oak table on the raised dais, Justin poked at his bowl full of oats. He yawned, put his head down on his left arm resting on the table, and with his spoon, sloshed milk against the side of the bowl.

"Eat up," Ash said, downing another mouthful. His bowl was almost empty.

Sighing, Justin set down his spoon. "I have eaten enough oats, Uncle."

Ash frowned. "Have you eaten *any*?"

"Aye."

"How many spoonfuls? One? Two?"

Sitting up, Justin set both arms on the table and grimaced. "I hate oats."

Ash resisted a chuckle; he'd hated eating oats as a boy, too. "They are very good for you. They will help you grow into a strong, skilled warrior." God above, but he sounded just like his father when Ash had been a child.

"What if I do not want to be a warrior? Does that mean I do not have to eat the oats?"

A silent groan welled within Ash. How in hellfire did he respond to questions like that? He didn't want to be a mean uncle, but he *did* want the boy to eat well and be fit for his training. Justin was old enough to learn the duties of a page, to start the years of training that would see him progress to being a squire, and then, one day, a knight. Ash's brother would have wanted his son to achieve knighthood— although Ash had believed it best not to enlist Justin as a page until the boy had adjusted to his new home and recovered from his sire's death.

When no good answer to Justin's questions came to mind, Ash shook his head and drew over the pot of honey. "Whatever you wish to be when you are a man, you will need your strength and good health. Therefore, you must eat your oats."

"But—"

"How about sweetening your portion with extra honey?"

Justin scowled. "I do not like too much sweetness."

"What about some more milk? That should make the spoonfuls easier to swallow."

"Naught will make them easier to swallow," Justin grumbled.

"Dried fruit, then? I will ask one of the maidservants to fetch some raisins and currants. How does that sound?"

The boy rolled his eyes. "Uncle…"

At the sound of boots crunching on the straw and

dried herbs strewn across the hall floor, Ash glanced up. A man-at-arms approached the dais. *What a timely interruption.*

"A missive for you, milord," the guard said.

'Twas early to be receiving a letter, unless the matter was urgent. Had Niles sent word of another discovery of ancient gold? Ash accepted the parchment from his soldier. "'Twas delivered today?" Ash asked.

"Moments ago," the man confirmed. "Delivered by a rider who did not stay to receive your reply."

The missive was sealed with wax bearing the imprint of a nobleman's ring. Ash's jaw hardened, for he recognized the design pressed into the dried wax. The note was from Edric.

He'd wondered how long it would take for the bastard to contact him.

Ash dismissed the man-at-arms, who bowed and strode away.

"A letter?" Justin asked, clearly intrigued. "Who is it from?"

"'Tis a matter of estate," Ash said, his chair scraping back as he rose. "Once you have finished your meal, I want you to practice a while with your bow."

Justin averted his gaze. "Do I really have to finish my oats?"

Ash patted the boy's shoulder. "You do." He winked and added, "If you eat the whole bowl full, I will tell you two stories about knights and damsels at bedtime tonight, not just one."

Justin grinned and snatched up his spoon.

Chuckling, Ash stepped down from the dais. Nodding to several folk who said good morning, he headed into the torch lit shadows of the forebuilding and down the stone steps to the door that opened into the bailey. He strode out into the morning breeze scented with the smells of baking bread and roasting fowl.

As the wind tugged at his hair and garments, he broke the seal on the parchment and read the note written in black ink:

Rosetta is missing. If you are in any way responsible, I will make you pay.

"Cooked oats with honey and milk, a mug of wine, and some bread and butter, milady." Herta crossed to the bedside and set the wooden tray on Rosetta's blanket-covered lap. "The cook even gave you some of her special plum jam. She makes it from fruit grown in the castle's orchard."

Sitting propped up against her pillows, Rosetta said, "It all looks delicious. Thank you." The fresh bread smelled heavenly.

"When you are done, I will help you dress. Your clothes, veil, and shoes are cleaned as thoroughly as they can be. I am afraid some of the stains in your gown will never come out. A shame, when 'tis made from such expensive silk."

Rosetta frowned. 'Twas Ash's fault that the exquisite gown was ruined; he had caused her to fall from her horse. However, Rosetta didn't see any sense in drawing Herta into what had happened in Clipston. "I see. Well—"

"The garments can still be worn, though. I just need to fetch them. One of the other maidservants would have brought them to the solar, but as I mentioned last night, three are unwell—told to stay in bed, I heard—and the week's orders just arrived from the miller, ale wife, and fishmonger. That means extra help is needed in the kitchens at the moment."

"I understand," Rosetta said. "Please thank the women who worked on my garments. I will be glad to have my own clothes to wear."

"I can imagine, milady. Did I mention that his lordship asked me to show you the gardens today? There are still a number of roses and other flowers in bloom, and on such a nice day, 'twill be a pleasant stroll."

Her mouth full of bread, Rosetta murmured her consent.

Herta beamed. "I will return as quickly as I can." She hurried out, leaving Rosetta to her meal.

After she'd finished eating, Rosetta set aside the tray and rose to wash her face and hands. She still had a bit of a headache, but 'twas far less intense than yesterday. The lump on her head wasn't as large or painful, either.

Last night, she'd returned the hairpins to the rest of the pile on the side table, and she'd tucked the eating dagger between the mattress and bed ropes. The weapon wasn't very accessible, though, under the bed. 'Twould be best if she could conceal the knife within her garments somehow.

She bent to retrieve the dagger, and the solar door opened.

"Here we are. Oh, and please do forgive me; I forgot to knock again." Herta hurried in, carrying Rosetta's shoes. The embroidered cloak, gown, and veil were draped over the young woman's arm. Seeing Rosetta quickly straighten from the side of the bed, Herta halted. "Milady? What are you doing?"

"Stretching," Rosetta said, bending at the waist to touch the bottom of the mattress and then straightening again. "I was still feeling a bit sleepy, and have been told that doing stretches is an excellent way to wake up in the morning."

The young woman looked uncertain.

Panic fluttered in Rosetta's breast—if Herta found the eating dagger, there would be no pleasant walk in the gardens—but she smiled and bent once more. "The stretches really do work. I am feeling much more awake, which is what I had hoped, for I do not wish to stumble or fall on our outing and get another bruise."

"O-of course, milady." Herta set the rustling heap of garments on the trestle table. "How much longer will you need for this…stretching?"

Rosetta reached her arms up to the beams overhead and then let them fall back to her sides. "I am done now."

Chatting non-stop while she worked, Herta helped Rosetta into her sheer lawn chemise and the exquisite, light-copper-colored gown Rosetta had worn on her ride into Clipston. The sensation of silk gliding against her skin, a tactile reminder of who she was, sent frissons of both relief and disquiet racing through Rosetta, for so much had happened yesterday. What were the coming days going to bring for her, Edric, and Ash?

There was so much she still didn't understand, including why Ash and Edric were no longer best friends. Edric had never mentioned his falling out with Ash to her. She'd have to ask Ash, then. After her many years of knowing them both, she surely deserved to know what had destroyed their friendship.

At last, Herta fashioned Rosetta's hair into a single braid and helped her don her shoes. Since the day was sunny and mild, Rosetta decided to forego the cloak. The young woman stepped back, looked her over from head to toe, and nodded briskly. "Lovely. Now, for that walk."

Herta opened the solar door and gestured for Rosetta to follow. Armed guards stood outside, but as Rosetta passed them, they nodded a polite greeting. Ash must have told them she was allowed out of her prison for a while.

The passageway, lit by flickering reed torches set into

iron brackets along both walls, led to a narrow wooden landing overlooking the great hall. As Rosetta descended the stairs, she took a quick glance around, her gaze skimming the heavy, carved table and chairs that dominated the raised stone dais, the whitewashed walls, and the orderly lines of trestle tables and accompanying benches that maidservants were scrubbing to a rich gleam. Even the straw and dried herbs scattered over the floor seemed clean—which made for a far more pleasant smell than she remembered from her visits to Edric's castle.

Herta led Rosetta through the hall, down the forebuilding stairs, and out into the bailey drenched in sunlight. Servants were busy with daily chores: washing clothes by the well; beating dust out of rugs with wooden paddles; grooming horses. Herta pointed out different folk and buildings of interest, until they came to a waist-high stone wall set with a wrought iron gate.

"I hope you like surprises," Herta said, lifting the latch on the gate.

Rosetta hesitated. Ash's kidnapping of her had certainly been a surprise. Did he have another unexpected event planned for her?

"That depends on the surprise," she answered.

Smiling, Herta preceded Rosetta into the garden.

While talking with a guard on his way to the gatehouse, Ash glanced over at the forebuilding. Herta and Rosetta were walking across the bailey. Rosetta's braided, golden hair gleamed in the sunshine, and she wore her own gown, the one he really hadn't paid much heed in the thrill of snatching her away from Edric. Now, Ash could only stare, the rest of his sentence fading to a stunned rasp, for he vowed she was the most captivating woman he'd ever seen.

The shimmering copper-colored silk of her dress hugged her bosom and waist and then flowed out into a sweeping fall that brushed the ground. Her sleeves also fit tightly to her arms and then flared at the hems, as must be the latest court fashion. Years ago, she'd told him how much she hated having to walk slowly and with elegance, as befitted a noblewoman; she'd much preferred running through fields and forests, splashing in the creek, and rolling in the verdant meadow grasses. Today, she nigh glided as she walked, as graceful and regal as a queen.

At the sound of a man—the guard he had been speaking to—clearing his throat, Ash snapped his attention back to the conversation. He didn't usually lose focus when ogling a woman. "Did I make my instructions clear?" Ash asked.

"Aye, milord." The guard bowed and walked off to his post.

Ash dragged his fingers through his hair and started for the keep. Reconsidering, he turned and strode for the stables. Last night, Justin had been concerned about one of the pups—the one he'd chosen for his own—and Ash wanted to be sure they were all thriving. The boy didn't need any more heartache to keep him from a good night's sleep; the lad hadn't had a full night of uninterrupted rest since he'd arrived at Damsley Keep.

The earthy scents of hay and horses enveloped Ash as he entered the shadowed interior. He nodded to the stable hands cleaning out the front stalls and headed to the rear of the building. The mother and her four pups, all latched onto her teats, lay on an old blanket in the end stall. Justin was there, too, kneeling beside them—not practicing his archery as Ash had instructed. The bow and quiver of arrows were lying on the straw a short distance from the boy.

Ash knelt beside the lad. "Justin."

The child didn't meet his gaze. "I wanted to see the puppies."

"You were supposed to practice with your bow. You assured me last night that you would, if I allowed you to keep one of the pups."

The boy's shoulders tightened, his posture clearly defiant. "I did eat all of my oats. You can ask the maidservant with the curly gray hair if you do not believe me."

Ash inwardly sighed. He did believe the lad; however, Justin needed to learn obedience. Obeying one's superiors without question was an essential part of chivalry, the code of honor that defined every part of a knight's life. "Justin—"

"I do not want to use my bow."

"Why not?"

"'Tis hard to nock the arrows."

"The more you practice, the easier 'twill become."

"I know, but—"

"'Twas not easy for me either, at first. When I was a boy, and my father gave me my first bow—"

"I just do not want to!"

At Justin's harsh words, the mother dog lifted her head and studied him. The puppies, jostled from their meal, whined and struggled to latch on again. With a frustrated sigh, the boy stroked the mother's head until she lay back on the blanket.

The boy's tenderness caused a warm ache to spread through Ash's chest. The lad's compassion was admirable. Justin's wellbeing, though, was important too.

"Look, Justin—"

The child clenched his hands into the straw. "Uncle, enough!"

Keeping his tone gentle but firm, Ash said, "You have seen the pups and found them all to be well. The one you were concerned about seems all right this morning, aye?"

The boy nodded.

"Now, you will go and spend some time with your bow."

Justin glowered. "I will not. I do not want to become a knight."

"Mayhap not at this moment, but you have the rest of your life to consider. I am your guardian and lord of this castle, and I want what is best for you not just for now, but years from now."

The boy's face reddened with anger, while tears glistened in his eyes.

Ash fought the overwhelming urge to yield; for the boy's own good, he must be taught the importance of obedience. "You will practice with your bow or there will be consequences. Go."

A sob wrenched from Justin as he lunged to his feet, snatched up his weapon and quiver, and ran out of the stall.

Ash sighed and bowed his head. He hoped he'd done the right thing, for he hated the guilt knotting up inside him.

The mother dog whined, and he patted her head before pushing to his feet. He would wait for Justin's temper to cool a little, and then they'd talk again. In the meantime, Ash had other responsibilities to attend, including Rosetta.

While she was out of the solar, likely wandering the garden with Herta by now, he would fetch a few items he needed, including the chess set. Ash made his way to his chamber and stepped inside, pleased to see the servants had tended to the fire and tidied the chamber.

His gaze slid to the made bed. *His* bed. Heat spread through his loins, for he wanted Rosetta in his bed every night, her slender body curled against his while he held her close.

Mentally forcing aside the tantalizing thought, he crossed to his linen chests and drew a ring of keys out of the bag tied to his belt. He opened the smaller chest to retrieve the roll of parchments.

As he did so, misgiving sifted through him. He stilled, his gaze traveling over the knives set on top his folded garments. The daggers were where he had left them, but not in the right order.

Someone had been through his belongings.

Chapter Seven

Rosetta had never seen such an exquisite garden. An orchard of apple, plum, and pear trees filled the section to the left of the gate; the thick, leafy boughs cast pleasant shade upon the ground below. Another area was devoted to orderly beds of vegetables and herbs. Herta led Rosetta across a grassy area dotted with wildflowers to where curving beds with knee-high, mortared stone walls ambled like the rose bushes they contained, drawing Rosetta and Herta down stone-covered paths to a pond covered in water lilies. Dragonflies and other insects dived across the water.

"Goodness," Rosetta said, sinking down onto the stone bench beside the pond. "There is a great deal to see." As she marveled at how much more elaborate this garden was than the one at Wallensford Keep—neither Edric's father nor Edric had seen a need to grow more than vegetables and herbs—a fish surfaced in the water and caused rings to ripple across the surface.

Chuckling, Herta sat beside Rosetta. "There is indeed. Our head gardener has maintained Damsley Keep's gardens for many years. He used to be a monk, but left monastic life after falling in love with a woman he met in a nearby town. She works in the castle's kitchens, along with their two sons."

"What a romantic story," Rosetta murmured.

"His lordship kept the gardens almost exactly as they were before he arrived, except for one addition."

"What addition is that?"

"I will show you."

Herta led Rosetta farther down the path. Through a surrounding wall of shoulder-high bushes, Rosetta saw upright stones, not as big as the ones she remembered, but still… "A stone circle," she breathed.

"The stones were once much larger. They had been removed from their original site and left by the side of a road. Most of the stones were broken, but his lordship took the best of what was left and had them brought here."

Rosetta wandered closer. Fourteen stones, just like the ancient structure on her father's lands. Two of the stones—just like the circle she remembered—were lying flat on the ground.

"Why did Lord Blakeley wish to recreate the stone circle?"

"He did not say," Herta answered. "I am told he visits here often. Mayhap it reminds him of his childhood?"

A flush warmed Rosetta's face. She and Ash had kissed for the first time at the stone circle on her sire's estate…

The afternoon sunlight gilded the ancient monument in an orange-yellow glow. As Rosetta wandered through the towering stones, her fingers skimming over the rough, weathered surfaces as she passed by, Ash stood like a victorious king on one that had toppled over and now laid flat on the ground.

"Do you ever wonder about the people who made this stone circle?" she asked, glancing back at him.

Hands on his hips, heedless of the dirt smudging his tunic, he shrugged. "Sometimes."

"They must have been very clever, to create a monument that is still standing to this day."

He jumped down from the fallen stone. "Clever? Like me?"

She giggled. "Well, to be honest..."

"Mmm?" He was right in front of her now; that reckless grin she loved so much curved his lips. A heady warmth fluttered inside her, for she'd loved every moment of the afternoon they had spent together. They'd shared a picnic spread out on a cloth on one of the fallen stones, wandered in the nearby field, watched the minnows darting through the creek, and she longed to show him how much he had come to mean to her. She, Edric, and Ash had been friends for years, but what she felt for Ash went beyond friendship.

"Ash," she began, not quite knowing how to say what she wanted. In the romantic stories they both loved, the knight always initiated the kiss with the maiden. Would Ash think her overly bold if she told him she longed for him to kiss her?

He stepped forward, claiming the space between them. As she gazed up at him, anticipation made her heart beat faster and her skin tingle as if icy raindrops had suddenly fallen from the clouds.

His mouth was so very close. Did she dare to rise up on tiptoes and press her lips to his? Oh, how she longed to! 'Twould be her very first kiss on the lips, and she wanted him to be the one...

He smiled, as if reading her thoughts. His head lowered. Holding very still, she waited, yearned.

His mouth touched hers.

Sensations raced through her: softness, warmth, and pleasure. Joy spread through her whole body, along with an incredible sense of lightness. She was floating, soaring, and as warm inside as sunlight, while he was stone, strong and enduring.

He lifted his mouth from hers, and their breaths mingled. "May I keep kissing you?" he whispered.

"I hope you will never stop," she answered.

His arm slid around her waist, drawing her in close. With a delighted sigh, she melted into the thrill of his kisses...

"...be heading back," Herta was saying. "The midday

meal will soon be served."

"A-all right." Rosetta tore her gaze from the standing stones and followed the maidservant back along the paths, wishing they could have stayed longer. Once Rosetta got back to the solar, though, she could—

A white cloth, stirring in the breeze, caught her attention. A table and two chairs had been set up on the grass, in the shade of the nearest fruit trees. Ash stood in the shadows. As she neared, he reached up, drew down a leafy branch, and picked an apple. The fabric of his tunic shifted, defining the sculpted, well-honed muscles of his shoulders and upper back. His male form was splendid, even if the mere sight of him made her quiver inside.

Her strides slowed, just as he faced her. He smiled and strode out of the shadows toward her, still holding the apple. He didn't walk like the gangly boy she'd once kissed. Ash's slow, swaggered strides warned her he'd grown into a man more than willing to risk all to get what he wanted, and who would not hesitate to tempt a woman he desired and then seduce her.

"You must be hungry after your walk," he said, tossing the apple up into the air and catching it. "Would you care for something to eat?"

Ash had ordered a simple meal: bread, cheese, pears, red wine, and some of the cook's special tarts filled with a buttery mix of dates, figs, and almonds. He'd set the apple he'd picked on the table between him and Rosetta, but so far, the fruit hadn't been eaten.

Truth be told, he could barely think about what he was putting in his mouth. He'd been looking forward to seeing Rosetta, to wooing her and earning more of her trust, and yet, his emotions churned, riled up by his disagreement with Justin and then finding out someone had been through his private possessions. While Ash didn't know with absolute certainty, he'd guessed that Rosetta had been the one who had broken into the smaller linen chest; the larger one, thankfully, had not been touched. He'd since removed both chests from the solar and locked them away in a guest chamber, but he still hadn't found his spare eating dagger.

Of even more concern was the fact she might have looked at the parchments that contained crown secrets. The information written on those pages was dangerous; divulged to the wrong people, it could even get her killed. He couldn't bear the thought that inadvertently, he had put her life in even more peril.

If he accomplished naught else today, he must find out whether or not she'd viewed the parchments—and if she had, he'd have to figure out how to rectify the situation.

Seated opposite him, Rosetta dined like a delicate bird, eating small morsels and taking care not to rush. He was in torment watching her slip the food into her mouth. He wanted to shove back his chair, lean over the table, and kiss her, to prove as he had last night that he still wanted her, and that she still wanted him too, even if she wouldn't admit it to herself.

Patience, his conscience reminded him. *To win her back, this time forever, you must have patience.*

"—enjoyed the stone circle," Rosetta was saying, still answering his question from moments ago about what she'd enjoyed most about the garden. Her keen blue gaze met his. "The structure looks just like the one we used to visit when we were younger."

"Indeed, it does."

"Why? What made you decide to copy it?"

My love for you, Briar Rose. Always, you.

He toyed with his uneaten tart, his gloved fingers knocking crumbs of the round pastry onto his plate. "'Twas a place I remembered from my youth, one that held…remarkable memories."

Remorse touched her gaze, swiftly veiled by the fall of her lashes.

Part of his pastry's shell collapsed; the delicacy was no longer perfectly whole, unblemished. An unexpected spark of anguish raced through Ash, and he removed his hand from the table and curled it into a fist under the drape of the linen cloth, even as Rosetta's attention shifted to his plate.

"When did you last visit the standing stones on your sire's lands?" Ash asked. A casual question, one she might expect in such a conversation, and yet, he eagerly awaited her answer. If other gold artifacts had been uncovered near the monument and reported to her sire, she might know about them. She might even have told her sire about the ring she'd found.

Rosetta wiped her mouth on a linen napkin and pushed aside her plate. "I have not been to the stone circle in years."

If gold had been discovered, mayhap her sire had forbidden folk to visit the site. "Why have you stayed away?"

She shrugged. "The place no longer held the same appeal once you and Edric were gone."

Ash gritted his teeth. How he hated her speaking of him and Edric in the same breath.

She studied him, a slight frown creasing her brow. "Why do you suddenly seem angry?"

If you only knew… "I was reminded of how much has changed since our days at Millenstowe Keep."

"I completely agree." Challenge glittered in her eyes, and his blood heated in acceptance of that challenge.

Dropping his gaze to the enticing swell of her bosom

accentuated by the close-fitting bodice, he murmured, "You are obviously no longer the girl—"

"I was referring to *you*, Ash. You are a man I barely recognize."

A harsh laugh broke from him. "I did not ask for my scars—"

"I do not mean your scars." Regret softened the heat of her stare. "I mean in your attitude, your actions…" A sound of frustration broke from her lips. "How long do you intend to keep me here? My parents will be frantic with worry. 'Tis not fair to them, Ash. And Edric—"

Ash hissed a breath.

"I would at least like to send my parents a missive to tell them that I am all right."

"I am sure you would," Ash muttered.

Her frown deepened. "Does that mean you agree to me sending a note?"

"When I believe circumstances warrant it, I will send a missive to your father."

"When, exactly, will that be? And what about Edric? Can I send him a missive, or are you going to make him worry, too?"

Edric again. Rage gathering inside him like winter storm, Ash leaned back in his chair. "I admire your concern for those you care about, Briar Rose. Surely, though, you should be more worried about yourself."

She folded her hands atop the table. "You might not be the same young lord I once knew, but I believe you are still a gallant knight governed by the rules of chivalry."

Ash's head dipped in acknowledgment. "True—"

"Therefore, despite your brazen act of kidnapping me, I do not believe you will mistreat me. Indeed, you would be very foolish to do so, since both my sire and my betrothed live within a few leagues of your castle and have strong armies. They will not hesitate to retaliate if I come to harm."

Ah, God, but she was extraordinary. Once again, she was a warrior queen, resolved to fight until her last breath. Smothering an admiring smile, he said, "Also true, but I was not referring to your being harmed."

Puzzlement crept into Rosetta's eyes. "Did you mean I should be thinking about finding a way to escape?"

He held her gaze, waited for the flicker of uncertainty he knew would appear. The breeze whispered through the tree boughs, the sound marking the strained silence between them.

"Very well," she conceded. What *did* you mean?"

"You must have known I would discover what you had done…although I still have not figured out exactly how you accomplished it. Hairpins, mayhap?"

Her face paled.

"You were very bold to go through my belongings."

"You were very bold to kidnap me."

He stared at her across the remnants of their meal. Judging by her glare, she wasn't going to back down. She was more likely to grab the apple and hurl it in his face, as she had done with the wine the other night. He really didn't want a black eye.

Ash reached over, picked up the fruit, and took a bite.

"If you expect me to apologize, Ash—"

He finished chewing the mouthful of crisp, juicy apple. "I would appreciate an apology. My linen chests were locked for good reason. However, since you now know what I have in my possession, there are crucial matters we must discuss."

Crucial matters. Judging by Ash's tone of voice, they were very important indeed.

She pushed her shoulders back as a shiver of dread rippled through her. She must remain strong. While she wouldn't normally have dared to go through his belongings—the lord of the castle's possessions—these weren't normal circumstances.

Whatever Ash wanted to talk about, she hoped she'd finally get some answers. If he tried to avoid divulging any information to her, she would persist. After all, if her mother were in such a predicament, she'd never yield.

Ash bit off more of the apple. Juice glistened on his lips. He was roguishly handsome even when he ate, which was most annoying. She looked away, wishing she could forget how wondrous she'd found his kisses—even the forbidden one last night.

He dropped the rest of the apple onto his plate. Glancing toward the keep, Ash rose and held out his hand to her. "Come."

She didn't move. "Why?"

"The breeze is strengthening. I do not want our words being carried to others who should not overhear."

A fair point. She rose, but pointedly ignored his hand.

He motioned to the stone path, and she walked alongside him as they strolled back through the rose beds. The blooms' fragrance wafted in the air, and she pushed aside memories of the bouquets of wild roses he'd given her years ago. Sometimes he had left a single bloom on her chair in Millenstowe Keep's great hall. He'd even left roses on her pillow, with notes saying he hoped she would dream about him all night. There had been no notes or roses, though, in the weeks since his return to England.

He led her to the bench by the fish pond and she sat, smoothing out her skirts. With a sigh, he sat down beside her, braced his arms on his knees, and leaned forward, his gaze on the water. How foolish that she was tempted to put her arm around his shoulders and rest her head against him, as she'd done so many times before.

"Do you remember that gold ring you found years ago?" Ash finally said, his hushed voice no louder than the hum of a swooping dragonfly.

"Of course."

He glanced at her. "Do you still have it?"

"Aye. 'Tis safely hidden." Meeting his gaze, she added, "I never told my father about it."

Ash nodded before looking back at the water. "Two days ago, another piece of ancient gold was found."

Shock jolted through her. "Was it more jewelry?"

"Nay, a coin. It bears similar designs, though, to what were on your ring."

"You would know," she said, "since you drew a copy of the ring."

A wry laugh broke from him. "So I guessed correctly. You did examine the parchments."

A sense of entrapment taunted her. He'd neatly backed her into that verbal corner—not that she would have lied if he had asked her directly. "I was curious—"

"Did you look at all of the parchments?"

"Aye."

"You do remember what you saw?"

"I do. You used to tease me about my good memory, remember?"

Shaking his head, he groaned. "Damnation, Briar Rose."

His obvious dismay made her breath hitch. "Mayhap I should not have read them, but I wanted to know…what you had done in the years since we parted."

"And what did you deduce from the parchments?"

She swept aside a dragonfly that had landed on her

skirts. "Not a great deal, except that someone had made a list of the names of a number of Warwickshire lords. 'Twas not a list you had compiled, though; I know your handwriting. I couldn't figure out the reason why those particular names, and not others, were on the list."

Ash picked up a rock from the ground and tossed it into the pond. Then, holding her gaze with an earnestness that pierced her straight to her soul, he said, "I wish you had not seen what was written on those documents. Now that you have, though—"

"—I should be told exactly what they mean," she finished. "I agree."

His expression shadowed with concern. "What I will tell you is not to be shared with anyone. I should not even be telling you. Do you understand?"

Excitement and misgiving warred within her. How wonderful that he trusted her enough to confide in her. Yet, what could be so crucial that she couldn't discuss it with anyone else? Had he discovered the location of a lost hoard of ancient treasure, to which her ring and the coin belonged? "If you insist, Ash, but—"

"I do insist." His hushed voice was a near growl. "Moreover, if you can elaborate upon what I tell you, you will not hesitate to share your knowledge with me. Agreed?"

She doubted she knew more about the riches than he did, but she nodded.

"The drawing," he began, "I made years ago because I believed that your ring was part of a vast trove. I felt 'twas important to document all aspects of the artifact, in case others were found—or your ring was lost or stolen."

"Have you found more gold? Do you know where the treasure is hidden?" she asked.

He shook his head. "The ring and coin are the only proof I have. Yet, there are tales that go back hundreds of years that tell of extraordinary riches to be found in these lands."

"I have heard some of those stories," she said. "My father told me about them when I was a child. When I asked about finding the treasure, he laughed and said that there was not likely anything left to find; any riches buried in the ground by ancient kings would have been dug up long ago. The tales have persisted, though, because they appeal to folk who dream of a better life."

Ash nodded. "I might have believed the stories were no more than folk tales, too, except for the ring and coin."

A sudden realization glimmered in her mind. "Do you intend to hunt for the riches?"

He chuckled, but the sound held no mirth. "To be honest, if there is a hoard nearby, I hope it remains hidden. 'Tis best for all of us if 'tis never found."

A distinct sense of danger threaded through his words, a caution that hinted at far more than the greed and squabbling that might accompany a discovery of lost riches. "What do you mean, best for all?"

He picked up another rock and threw it; it landed in the water with a *plonk*. "Do you follow any of the London politics?"

"Not really. I am aware, though, that with King Richard fighting in the East, England is being governed by men who are loyal to him."

Ash's attention shifted to her. "Some of them are loyal. Others would much rather see his brother, John Lackland, take control of the English throne."

She gasped. "You speak of treason."

"Aye, although the traitors lack one important element: funding. However, if they were to come into possession of ancient riches, and use the gold to pay for weapons and mercenaries—"

"They could seize the throne."

"Exactly."

Oh, mercy! Her pulse hammered. "With King Richard so far away—"

"—he would not be able to stop the takeover. 'Tis why we are doing what we can to keep John Lackland from power."

She sat very still. Her head reeled with the implications of what he'd told her. "You said '*we* are doing what we can.' Obviously, that includes you. Does it also include the lords named on that parchment in your linen chest?"

"Regrettably, nay." Ash brushed dirt from his fingers. "Those men are known to be supporters of Lackland."

Chapter Eight

Ash held Rosetta's stare, refusing to look away, while her eyes filled with dismay. He yearned to take her in his arms, to hold her, to whisper words of comfort while she wrestled with the knowledge that Edric had forsaken their King.

"Ash…" Her fingers curled on the edge of the stone bench, as if she tried to keep herself from toppling to the ground. "Are you certain?"

"If a lord's name is on the list, he is a traitor."

"But Edric—"

"Including Edric," Ash said.

She shook her head, her skin suddenly ashen. "You both fought alongside King Richard on Crusade. If Edric had not supported the King, he would not have gone."

"He was loyal when he left England. Men change, though, after going to war. He…" Ah, God, but the damning words clogged Ash's throat, refused to be voiced. He'd already shocked her enough for one day, and he didn't want her to grow to hate him.

She had gone rigid beside him, though, her demeanor clearly one of stubborn denial.

"What proof do you—or the person who wrote that

list—have against Edric?" she asked, her words crisp.

"My informant who lives nearby—"

"*Informant*? You are a spy?"

"Aye. King Richard visited me while I was recovering from my wounds and told me what would be required of me. I agreed, and confirmed my appointment to his group of spies with a solemn oath."

"That explains your garments, then. I had wondered why so many were plain and rather ordinary for a nobleman."

Ash chuckled. "I had not realized you had examined my clothing so carefully. I am flattered you cared enough to notice."

"Believe me, there are a great many things I have noticed about you," she murmured.

He winked. "Good things, I hope."

Rosetta glanced down the path winding through the rose beds, as if such a thought weren't even worth considering. He tamped down a flare of remorse, refusing to let his emotions complicate their important conversation.

"I asked about proof," she reminded him. "What do you have that incriminates Edric?"

"I would like to tell you, even show you, but I cannot."

Her gaze sharpened. "I remember there were dates and places mentioned on the list, along with the names."

"Mmm." Ash brushed away a bit of straw clinging to his hose, a reminder of his earlier conversation with Justin.

The weight of her stare bored into him. "Ash, why will you not tell me? You have confided to me other information that you considered to be highly secret."

He met her gaze. "I have, but only because you broke into my linen chest and left me no other choice. The knowledge you have now is dangerous enough. I will not increase the risk of peril to you by telling you more."

She studied him, both hurt and astonishment glimmering in her eyes. "Without proof, 'tis difficult for me to believe that Edric—"

"I know. You must trust me, though."

"Must I? All I have to go by is your word."

"What I have told you *is* the truth."

Her white-knuckled fingers tightened further on the bench. He longed to capture her closest hand, bring it to his lips, and kiss it, for he hated to see her so distressed. After a silence, she asked, "Is that why you kidnapped me? Because you did not want me to become the wife of a traitor?"

Ribbons of regret and rage wrapped around Ash's heart. "'Tis one of the reasons."

"And the others?"

The others. He exhaled a sharp breath, and his gut twisted. She already doubted what he'd told her about Edric. To tell her the most wretched of the revelations now—

The gritty sound of someone walking on the path carried on the breeze. Ash straightened, to see Herta hurrying toward them.

"Milord," she called. "You have a visitor. He said the matter is urgent."

Rosetta strolled down the paths between the vegetable and herb beds. After promising that she wouldn't try to escape—fleeing wasn't possible, Ash had warned her, with the number of guards he had stationed at the gatehouse and on the battlements—he'd allowed her to stay in the garden while he met with his visitor. Herta had gone to finish an errand, leaving Rosetta to wander on her own.

Truth be told, Rosetta was glad of the chance to be

alone. Troubling thoughts crowded her mind; they jostled and shoved, demanding to be acknowledged. As she walked, rubbing her aching brow, starlings twittered from atop the tied posts to her left that had supported beans earlier in the season. In the vegetable bed to her right, rows of leeks and onions grew alongside lettuces that had gone to seed. A sense of order prevailed in the neat rows and tidy, stone-bordered beds—such a contrast to the chaos in her mind.

How could Edric be a traitor? She simply couldn't believe that of him. While he had his faults—a quick temper among them—she couldn't recall any instances when she'd ever had reason to doubt his loyalty to the crown. Aye, he was gone from Wallensford Keep for days at a time now and again, but that was true of most lords. She remembered her father being away often when she was young; he'd inspected different parts of his estate and visited other noblemen and even traveled to London for important meetings with crown officials.

She also recalled that as a young lad, Edric had trained for long days to become worthy of knighthood. He'd been proud to serve his King in faraway lands. Ash had said that men changed after being in battle—and Ash himself was proof that men did—but what could have happened to make Edric forsake his pledge to the crown and support a rebellion?

The breeze stirred the boughs of the nearby fruit trees, the sound akin to a hiss. She hugged herself and shivered. Her jumbled mind must be playing tricks on her, for she would swear someone was watching her. Yet, she hadn't seen anyone else in the garden.

Rosetta walked on through shadows splintered by the sunshine slanting down through the trees. She picked a sprig of rosemary and rubbed the fragrant herb between her fingers to savor the smell—

A twig snapped to her left. She spun, her gaze

searching beneath the trees. "Is someone there?" Ash had loved to creep up on her and startle her when they were younger; was he up to such mischief now? "Ash?" she called. "Is that you?"

The tree leaves rustled in the breeze. No one answered.

Shaking her head, she continued her walk. Again, she felt someone watching her. Either she was losing her mind or whoever was spying on her was hiding. She smiled, for if 'twas Ash, she would best him at his own game.

Rosetta walked on a few more leisurely paces, and then swiftly turned. With a startled squawk, a young boy darted behind the trunk of a tree.

So she *had* been spied upon. Not by Ash, though.

She remained where she was until the lad peeked around the tree. Their gazes met, and he retreated again. He must be very shy...or mayhap he wasn't supposed to be in the garden? Either way, she was intrigued.

"You, behind the tree," she said. "I do hope you asked the garden sprites if 'tis all right for you to hide there."

The boy, clearly curious, peered out from behind the trunk.

"If you did not ask..." She whistled. "They can be very grumpy, and if they get upset, they get hungry for children."

Wide-eyed, the boy stepped out from his hiding place. He must be a son of one of the servants. His dark blond hair was overly long and unkempt, his face was dotted with freckles, and his pewter gray tunic was filthy. His hose were also too short and covered with bits of straw. "I have never heard of garden sprites before," he said.

"They are secretive creatures. Few folk ever see them."

"Do they *really* eat children?"

"They do. Those stories you might have heard about

boys going outside to play and then vanishing, never to be seen again? They were gobbled up by garden sprites."

Concern lit the lad's gaze. "I had no idea."

"They especially like boys with dark blond hair, for they taste especially delicious."

Shock etched his features, and then he grinned. "You are teasing me."

She laughed. "I am. At least I get to talk to you now."

He moved closer, his eyes bright with interest. "Are you the lady?"

"The lady?" she asked.

"The special guest who is staying in the solar."

She smothered the urge to say that she was not a guest, but had been brought to the castle against her will.

"My uncle said you are very beautiful. He was right."

She blushed. Whoever his relative was—one of the guards outside the solar, mayhap?—she'd obviously made an impression upon him. "'Twas most kind of your uncle. I am indeed the lady from the solar. My name is Rosetta Montgomery. And you are?"

"Justin." He bowed, almost losing his balance. Wrinkling his freckled nose, he said, "I hope my uncle does not find out that I have trouble bowing. He will make me practice until I get it right."

"Does your uncle live at the keep?"

Justin nodded before glancing over his shoulder, as though worried he might find his dreaded relative drawing near. "I am supposed to be practicing my archery, but I do not feel like it. I would rather do what *I* want to do."

A pang of sympathy trailed through her. While she understood the boy's reluctance, it sounded as though his uncle was encouraging him to become a soldier, an honorable way of life for any young man. There was a demand for skilled fighters at every castle; he would earn a good living.

Mayhap, in her own small way, she could help his uncle. "Can I see your bow?" she asked.

Justin frowned. "Why, milady?"

"My father has one made from yew. 'Twas given to him by his sire, and 'tis one of his prized weapons."

His shoulders hunched, Justin walked to a tree several paces away and returned with a bow and quiver of arrows. The small bow was of fine quality and appeared to have been made just for him. What a shame, that his uncle had spent hard-earned coin on a weapon the boy didn't want to use.

She took one of the arrows from Justin's quiver and tried to fit the feathered end to the string. She'd attempted to use a bow before—Ash and Edric had offered to teach her one autumn afternoon—but she hadn't been any good at it. They'd collapsed on the ground laughing, and she had promptly given up. Fumbling, she said, "How does it—?"

"I will show you." Justin took the bow and nocked the arrow.

"Oh, I see." She tapped her chin with a finger. "That looks right, but how do you shoot it?"

"Like this." The boy sighted down the arrow, drew it back along with the string, and fired. The arrow landed in the grass a fair distance away.

"Well done," she said, clapping.

Justin shrugged, but seemed pleased by her praise. "I did not hit a target."

"Nay, but I did not ask you do. Can you fire another arrow, so I can be sure to remember what you did?"

"I can." Suspicion crept into his gaze. "Do noblewomen ever use bows? I thought knights protected ladies, as is their duty."

"Usually chivalrous knights do protect ladies," Rosetta agreed. "However, in the middle of a siege, knights are usually busy defending the castle or battling enemy warriors. That means ladies sometimes have to protect themselves. I certainly would rather know how to use a weapon than be trapped and helpless."

The boy nodded. He suddenly seemed to grow a little taller, for he pushed back his shoulders and drew another arrow from his quiver. "Fear not, milady. I will do my best to teach you all I know."

"Lord Sherborne's men have gone through every building in Clipston from roof to cellar," Niles said, his voice hushed as he leaned forward in his chair by the great hall's hearth. "He is searching for his bride who disappeared on her way to the church, as well as a rider wearing a black helm and cloak. So far, neither has been found."

Lounging in the other chair by the fire, Ash brushed his hand over his mouth to hide a smile. He'd thrown the helm and cloak into a river on the ride back to Damsley Keep with Rosetta. Even if Edric suspected that Ash had abducted her, the bastard would never find solid proof.

"Is Sherborne still searching?" Ash asked. How he'd love to be able to witness Edric's rage and frustration.

"His lordship has returned to Wallensford Keep, but his men-at-arms continue to walk the town streets. A considerable reward has been posted for information on the horseman that will lead to his capture. There are rumors, you see, that he kidnapped Lady Montgomery to keep the wedding from taking place."

"Who would dare to do such a thing?" Ash did his very best to appear shocked.

Niles shook his head. "The man must have ballocks of steel."

Ballocks of steel? Ash fought a grin.

"He has offended both the lady's sire and Lord Sherborne," Niles continued. "Her kin are not people a man would want to cross either."

A log shifted in the hearth, sending up a swirl of red sparks. "Do they have any leads on the abductor?" Ash asked, watching the blaze.

"A few, but the reward has created even more havoc. Townsfolk are pointing fingers at neighbors and friends alike." His gaze narrowing, Niles said, "You would not know the whereabouts of the missing lady, would you?"

Ash kept his expression neutral. "What makes you ask such a question?"

"You and Sherborne were once good friends, were you not? Lady Montgomery knew both of you, and, so I have heard, was especially close to you?"

"Your point?" Ash asked, careful to neither deny nor confirm Niles' words.

"Well, I thought with you returning to England, she might have contacted you—"

"I did receive a few letters from her," Ash said with a shrug, "but I never replied to them. 'Tis as much written communication as she and I have shared. Now, what is this urgent matter that brought you here? Surely 'tis more than the search for Lady Montgomery?"

Niles studied Ash for a long moment, and then his focus shifted back to the fire. "I have news of more gold."

Ash's heart kicked against his ribs. "Dug up in the same area?"

"I am not certain where 'twas discovered, milord. I was in a tavern on the outskirts of Clipston, waiting for a friend to meet me for a drink, when I heard two men at the table behind me talk about the gold coin that the peasant had found. They seemed to have heard of it through local gossip. Then the men mentioned a gold belt buckle that had been dug up in a field. The farmer who found it vanished a day later. All of his possessions were still in his home, and his wife reported him missing, so he had not moved away. His corpse was found in the forest a couple of days later. The men believed he was killed for the gold."

"When was the belt buckle found?" Ash asked, anticipation running hot in his blood.

"From what I could gather, mayhap a few months ago, although the men did not say exactly when. My friend arrived and, while I wanted to hear more, the men soon rose and left."

A ring, a coin, and a belt buckle. There could be no doubt about lost treasure nearby.

"I am right about that gold from the Kingdom of Mercia," Niles said, his eyes glinting in the fire glow. "We *must* find it before the King's enemies."

"I agree," Ash said. "I pray we are not already too late."

Chapter Nine

"I still cannot believe that I am betrothed." Herta held out her left hand yet again to admire the plain silver band set with a small blue bead. "I feel as if I am in a dream."

Rosetta smiled. "You are not dreaming, I promise you."

"Oh, milady." The young woman's eyes shone. "I am so excited. I am not going to be able to sleep tonight. My mind will be whirling with all of the arrangements that must be made."

While Herta had been finishing her errand that afternoon, her suitor, one of the stable hands, had found her, taken her to a quiet spot by the tiltyards, and asked her to marry him. She'd said aye. Thrilled and completely in love, Herta had talked of nothing but her betrothal as soon as she'd entered the solar.

Herta now gestured to the chair near the hearth, and Rosetta sat so that the young woman could take out her braid. Rosetta had spent most of the afternoon in the garden, staying there long after Justin had grown tired of his archery and left. She'd only returned to the keep a short while ago and had declined Ash's invitation to dine with him. She simply didn't feel up to the noise and activity of the great hall while she was still struggling to accept all that he had told her earlier. Herta had brought her a plate of bread, cheese, and cold meats that Rosetta hadn't yet eaten. The young woman had also ordered Rosetta a bath that would arrive once the water had been heated.

"Were you as thrilled the day you got betrothed, milady?" Herta asked, moving to stand behind Rosetta. The young woman began working on Rosetta's tresses.

Rosetta turned the emerald and pearl ring on her finger. The extravagant jewel almost seemed to make a mockery of her betrothal when compared to Herta's small ring that had been given, and accepted, with so much joy and love. "My situation was a little different from yours."

"Different, milady? In what way?"

I didn't love Edric, but I chose to accept his proposal anyway. "I agreed to marry Edric in part to protect my father's lands. Edric's and my sire's estates border one another, you see. The marriage will allow the lands to be joined once my father has died." As Herta ran the brush through her loosened hair, Rosetta added, "Father is in excellent health, so 'twill not be for a long while yet."

"I have heard of such marriages, milady—ones intended to secure inheritances and preserve family fortunes."

A note of sympathy softened the young woman's voice, and Rosetta fought a pang of envy. Herta was lucky to be able to marry the man she adored, and to be free of the obligations that came with being born into a titled family. "Such nuptials are very common for noblewomen," Rosetta admitted. "Some ladies are married when they are still children, not even old enough to bear heirs. At least Edric and I are of a similar age and know one another well. We have been friends since we were young."

"A strong friendship makes for a fine marriage,

milady." The brush made a soothing, whispering sound as it skimmed through Rosetta's hair.

"True," Rosetta said. "I feel very fortunate to be wedding a man I know, rather than a complete stranger. My parents did not know one another before their marriage was arranged by the crown. I cannot imagine what that must have been like for them."

"Oh, I agree, milady."

"Edric is not perfect, but I could do far worse for a husband."

"I am dying to know... Is he handsome?" Herta asked, her tone brightened with mischief.

Rosetta chuckled. "He is. What about your fiancé?"

"He is less handsome than some, but he makes up for that with his quick wit and easy laughter." The young woman sighed blissfully. "He will be a good husband to me and a fine father to the children we will have together. Those are the things that matter to me."

Envy poked at Rosetta again. What mattered most to the noble elite was producing heirs. She would be honor-bound to give Edric at least one strong, healthy son.

"Your lord," Herta said, continuing her brushing. "Would you say he is as handsome as Lord Blakeley?"

A startled tremor rippled through Rosetta. "Well—"

"His lordship might have his scars, but he is still a very becoming man," Herta murmured. "Do you not agree?"

Completely.

Rosetta brushed a crease from her skirt. "I have not really noticed—"

"Milady!" Herta giggled. "Every other woman in Damsley Keep has noticed. He certainly admires you. Have you not seen the way he looks at you?"

Heat warmed Rosetta's face. She did *not* want to be drawn into a discussion of her feelings for Ash.

"'Tis a shame that you are already betrothed, Lady

Montgomery, for I vow you and he would be well suited."

"Herta, please—"

"Oh, I am sorry, milady, I know 'tis not my place to say such things. I will say no more, but I do hope his lordship will find a beautiful woman like you to be his wife. He deserves happiness and—"

Muffled voices came from outside the solar.

"Excuse me a moment." Herta set down the brush and hurried to the doorway. After speaking to someone outside, the young woman said, "Your bath is here, milady."

"Thank you." Rosetta hugged herself, for she couldn't wait to sink into the warm water. Naught soothed frayed nerves better than a bath, and with all that Ash had told her still haunting her thoughts, Rosetta needed a long soak to help calm her mind.

Servants entered carrying a round, wooden bathing tub which they set by the hearth. More lads followed with buckets of steaming water. Once the tub was filled, Herta shut the door, her arms laden with linen towels, a washcloth, and a fresh cake of soap. Setting the items beside the tub, she said, "I will help you undress milady, and then will give you a nice scrubbing. I will wash your hair too, shall I?"

"'Tis kind of you to offer, Herta, but I can manage on my own."

The young woman's eyes widened. "His lordship would expect me to assist you."

"Truly, I will be fine. I usually bathe on my own." Rosetta took the items from Herta's arms. "Why not go and find your fiancé and celebrate your exciting news with your friends?"

Herta blushed. "Well…all right, milady."

Once Herta had left, Rosetta slipped off her gown and chemise and left them in a heap on the floor. Herta had closed the shutters at the window a short while ago, blocking out the twilight sky and cooling breeze, but the air in the solar still held a draft, causing goose bumps to rise on Rosetta's arms. Naked, she stepped into the tub and sank into the water. She closed her eyes on a long sigh. *Heaven.*

Droplets pattered onto the water's surface as she moistened the soap and washcloth and thoroughly scrubbed her face, arms, and legs. The ritual of washing away the day's strain was marvelously soothing...although part of her couldn't help wondering if Ash used this same tub. Had he bathed near the hearth in this chamber, as she was doing now? How wicked that she could easily imagine him dragging a soapy cloth over his broad, rippling chest and leaving behind a trail of foamy white bubbles. His skin would glisten like oiled bronze in the firelight. His dark hair would cling to his strong, wet cheekbones as he—

Rosetta tossed the washcloth into the water that had turned a milky hue from the soap. This might be Ash's castle, and his private room, but he was *not* going to intrude on her bath. Seeing that buckets of water had been left for her to rinse her hair once she'd washed it, Rosetta pushed her tresses back from her face, closed her eyes, and then submerged.

As the depths surrounded her, she surrendered to the cocooning warmth.

"I met the lady today."

Ash glanced at Justin, seated beside him at the lord's table. Over the buzz of noise from the rest of the folk eating in the great hall, Ash said, "Did you, now?" He'd tried his best not to sound surprised and a bit annoyed. After their argument in the stable, Ash had expected the boy to have gone straight to the tiltyards to practice with his weapon.

The boy spooned up another mouthful of pottage, while Ash chewed a piece of buttered bread. "Her name is Lady Montgomery. She is very nice. And pretty."

A wry laugh broke from Ash. His Briar Rose had clearly won over this young lad. "Where did you meet her?"

"In the garden. She asked to see my bow." The boy stuffed more pottage into his mouth. Ash had never seen Justin with such an appetite.

"I see. Did you show the bow to her?" Ash ate more bread that he'd dipped into the pottage broth.

Justin nodded and wiped his mouth—on his dirty sleeve, of all places. Ash cringed and pushed a linen napkin toward the boy, who dutifully wiped his lips a second time. "She tried to fire an arrow, but she was hopeless at it. She is a lady, after all."

Reaching for his wine, Ash downed a quick mouthful to suppress a laugh. He could imagine how indignant Rosetta would be if she heard such things said about her.

"I showed her what to do," the boy continued. "She liked seeing me shoot the arrows, so I did some practicing while she watched."

Shock rippled through Ash, along with a flare of admiration. Thanks to her, the boy had completed his weapons practice for the day and, it seemed, had enjoyed it.

He patted Justin's arm. "Well done. I am proud of you."

"Really?" Such hope shone in the boy's eyes.

"Really."

Justin set down his spoon, rose, and threw his arms around Ash. "I am glad," the boy whispered against Ash's neck. "I do not like it when you are upset with me."

Ash's heart constricted, and his arms instinctively tightened around the boy who smelled of earth and fresh air. Ash didn't like being upset with Justin, either. He held the child, reluctant to break the emotional bond that had suddenly grown between them.

At last, the boy drew away, rubbing at his eyes. Dropping down in his chair again, he wrinkled his nose at the dregs of his pottage. "Have I eaten enough for tonight?"

"You have. Why do you not go and check on the puppies?"

Justin grinned. His chair scraped back as he leapt to his feet and hurried from the hall.

Smiling, Ash watched him go. At least they had resolved their disagreement—thanks to Rosetta. Thinking of her, how lovely she'd looked in the garden, roused a stirring of longing within him. He wanted to see her. He *needed* to see her.

Ash left the table and climbed the stairs up to the landing and the corridor leading to the solar. He greeted the guards outside the door, halted, and knocked.

No answer.

Ash frowned. Rosetta had no doubt recognized his knock. Was she purposefully ignoring him? She *had* refused to dine with him that evening, no doubt because she hadn't liked what he had told her in the garden.

He knocked again.

Still no reply.

This was *his* castle. Even if she was upset with him, or indisposed, she should still acknowledge him.

He shoved down the iron handle and strode in.

The solar was still and quiet. As he pushed the door shut behind him, he thought she wasn't in the room, but then he saw the bathing tub and her submerged in the cloudy water.

She surfaced, gasping, her eyes still closed and water pouring down her face. He could only stare, enraptured, as she tilted her head back and smoothed her tresses away from her cheeks. In the firelight, her fair skin glistened. The fire glow flickered over her sleek nakedness, luring his gaze down to the slope of her throat and shoulders, and then even farther down, to the tantalizing roundness of her pink-tipped breasts.

He couldn't breathe. He couldn't move. God's holy blood, but she was even more exquisite than he'd imagined in his dreams. Hot, heady desire filled his veins.

She blinked. As if suddenly realizing she was no longer alone, her gaze flew to him.

"Ash!" She dropped down into the water, until only her face was visible above the surface. "H-how dare you!"

Chapter Ten

"Of course I dare, Briar Rose," Ash said with a lazy grin. "This *is* my solar."

Rosetta stared up at him from the edge of the tub, while the water continued to lap against her from her quick retreat into its depths; some of the bathwater had even splashed onto the planks and soaked the rug.

True, 'twas his chamber, and as lord, he had every right to come and go as he pleased. Surely he had more respect for her, though, than to stride in while she was bathing and therefore naked?

"I did knock," he said, as if that explained how he'd come to be standing just a few paces away from the tub. "You obviously did not hear me."

"Obviously," she muttered. What was she going to do *now?* She wished she could lift her hand and wipe away the droplets running into her eyes, but she couldn't move without him seeing even more of her than a lady ever revealed to a man except when she was married to him and in the privacy of their bedchamber.

Except that this was *his* bedchamber, and once, long ago, they'd talked about running away and getting married…

Ash's gaze slid down to her chin touching the rim of the tub. His eyes smoldered, and she shuddered in the water that was rapidly lost its warmth.

"What reason did you have for disturbing me, Ash? As you can see, I am not prepared for visitors."

"I guessed that." He winked. "For some reason, though, I find myself reluctant to be gallant and leave."

Heat spread across her face at his husky tone. She shouldn't be flattered by his roguishness, and yet, a delicious, wanton heat chased through her, right down to the tips of her toes.

His wicked grin widening, he closed the distance between them and crouched in front of her, the leather of his boots creaking.

His expression was a heart-wrenching blend of fierce longing and self-restraint. Long ago, he'd gazed upon her in such a manner. Her pulse thundered, excitement and remorse tangling up inside her like fast-growing vines.

The scent of him, of the outdoors, leather, and man, teased her over the lingering fragrance of the soap she'd used to wash. As he reached out and gently brushed water droplets from her cheek, a nagging pressure spread through her lower belly—a forbidden desire she was finding more and more difficult to suppress.

"Do you have any idea how I have dreamed of seeing you naked?" he whispered, his gloved finger sliding along her cheekbone.

"Ash—"

"I still dream." His finger glided over her mouth, and the softness of the leather against her lips made her shudder. "I am sure, though, that what I imagine is nowhere near as lovely as you really are."

How she ached inside to hear such words. Even as she acknowledged her own yearning for him, however, her gaze slid to the ring on her hand.

Ash's focus shifted to the jewel, too. He exhaled a harsh breath, shoved to standing, and turned his back to her.

She sighed, a sound of regret as well as relief.

"Believe it or not, I did come here with a good reason for seeing you," he said. "I came to ask…if you would like to walk with me on the battlements."

Rosetta glanced at his back, her gaze indulging in a quick study of his broad shoulders, narrowed waist defined by his leather belt, and strong, muscular legs. So handsome, and yet, still a mystery to her in a great many ways.

Mayhap 'twas best for them both, when the attraction between them was still undeniably real. The better she knew him, the harder 'twould be to forget him when she left Damsley Keep. She was already practically married to Edric, apart from the formal church ceremony. Yet, even as the rational part of her mind encouraged her to refuse Ash's offer of a walk, her conscience reminded her that she'd loved him once; he'd been her best friend as well as her soul mate, and she owed it to their past friendship to try and at least understand the warrior he had become. "I would enjoy a walk," she said.

"Tell the guards when you are ready. All right?" Ash's head turned slightly, revealing his sun-bronzed profile to her.

"All right."

"I will see you anon."

He left, the door shutting behind him.

Rosetta finished washing her hair and then stood, water streaming down her body. She grabbed one of the linen towels and dried her torso, then twisted her hair up in the towel before stepping out of the tub and drying off her legs and feet. Shivering in the cool air, she donned her chemise and silk gown, combed out her wet hair, slipped on her shoes, and then drew on her cloak. She tapped on the door.

A guard answered. His features reminded her of

Justin. Was he the boy's uncle? She was tempted to ask; however, she didn't want the lad to think she had been talking about him with his relative.

"I will summon Lord Blakeley for you, milady," the man said, bowing.

"Thank you."

While she waited, she sat by the fire, running the brush through her tresses. Her hair was almost dry when she heard Ash's familiar knock.

She crossed to the door just as he entered. His gaze skimmed over her, and his mouth curved in a wolfish smile that swept her back to a short while ago when she'd been naked.

"Enough, Ash," she muttered.

He chuckled and gestured for her to step out into the shadowed, torch lit passageway. "What I saw earlier?" he said while they walked side by side. "'Twas far from enough to satisfy my lustful curiosity."

Mercy, but that wanton thrill shot through her again. With effort, she stifled it.

He escorted her to a doorway opening onto a flight of stone steps leading up. He urged her to go first, while he followed close behind. When her foot slipped on the uneven stairs, he steadied her, one hand at her waist and the other holding her hand, until she regained her balance. 'Twas odd to touch his fingers encased in leather, rather than his bare skin. With a twinge of regret, she wished he would trust her enough to let her see his injured hands.

The stairs opened onto the battlements where a few burning torches cast light into the darkness. Stars glinted in the black sky overhead, and the wind whispered across the weathered stonework as they walked together to the crenellated wall.

"'Tis a beautiful night," she said, hugging herself. "The stars are as bright as gems."

"We used to sneak away from the great hall and go up to the battlements of Millenstowe Keep to watch the stars," Ash murmured. "Do you remember?"

"I do." She recalled everything about those glorious days with him. They had watched the night sky while she'd stood in his embrace, her back pressed against his chest, her head tipped back against his shoulder. She had never felt closer to him than in those moments. His love for her, and hers for him, had wrapped around them like a cozy blanket and she'd been safe, content, and so very sure that she never wanted to be anywhere else but with him.

Tears pricked her eyes, and she walked away a few paces, fighting to regain control of her emotions.

He followed, his boots rapping on the stone. "Briar Rose."

She paused by a stone merlon and turned her face into the wind. It blew strands of hair into her face and she shut her eyes, glad of the chance to hide her brimming tears.

Leather rasped against her cheek as he eased the hair away.

Her eyes fluttered open to find Ash staring down at her. The sadness in his gaze caused a painful pressure to gather within her. "Ash—"

"I wish I could touch you," he whispered. "Rip off this damned leather and *really* touch you. I remember the softness of your skin. 'Tis like the finest goose down. And the silk of your hair... 'Tis like the most expensive cloth."

"If you remove your gloves—"

"*Never.*"

"Why not? Your scars are marks of honor."

"I cannot—"

"Ash, you got your wounds while fighting for the King. They are proof of your life's experiences, and part of who you are now. They are naught to be ashamed of."

Wariness and pain etched his features. "You would

not know. You have not seen my hands."

"I *want* to see them. Truly I do. I need…"

"Need?" The huskiness of his tone made her tremble inside. "What do you need, Briar Rose?"

You, the way you were before, when love between us was as natural as breathing.

"I want to at least understand why you are the man you have become." The words sounded awkward, strained, but at least she'd finally said them.

He stared out into the night, his demeanor unyielding.

Lowering her voice, she said, "I know there are things you cannot tell me, because of what you do for the crown. Yet, every time you speak of Edric—"

Ash cursed.

"See? You get angry."

"As is my *right*."

"Why? What happened between you two? I simply do not—"

"Understand?" Such hatred flashed in Ash's eyes: anger not for what she'd asked, but for what he knew and she didn't.

"Aye," she said softly.

"If I tell you the truth, you will not believe me."

"Ash!"

He leaned in closer in the darkness, his breath rasping across her brow. "In regards to what happened? I cannot even prove the truth to you or anyone else. How do you think that makes me feel?"

"Knowing the truth while others are oblivious to it… 'Tis a terrible burden to carry on your own."

His eyes flared with surprise, and then he averted his gaze.

"I want the truth," she insisted. "I do not care how difficult it might be to hear."

His expression bleak, Ash said, "Once I have said the words, I cannot take them back."

"I know."

Anguish shivered across his face. His voice like grating stone, he said, "My forehead and hands were cut by an enemy sword. However, I was not wounded while battling a Saracen."

Confusion rippled through her. "Then how—?"

"I was attacked by a man I trusted and loved as a brother."

"You cannot mean—"

"Aye, Briar Rose. Edric used the weapon on me."

Chapter Eleven

orror lashed through Rosetta; it broke from her in a low, despairing cry ripped from her soul. "*Edric* attacked you?"

"Aye."

A violent tremor rippled through Rosetta. Her legs suddenly went weak, and she turned to lean back against the nearest stone merlon, glad of its solid strength to hold her upright. "W-why would he do such an awful thing?"

"Because…" Ash sighed, the sound ragged. "He did not want me to have you."

The tears Rosetta had fought so hard to hold back filled her eyes. "Oh, Ash—"

"He had always been jealous of our love. While he and I journeyed to the East, he teased me about having to end my relationship with you in order to go on Crusade. He called it the choice between my maiden and my King."

Tears trailed down her cheeks.

"Edric vowed that since I had broken your heart, you were forever lost to me. When he returned from Crusade, he intended to ask your father for your hand in marriage."

"Ash," she moaned. She'd been aware of Edric's jealousy, but had never paid it too much heed.

"I tolerated Edric's teasing because, in many other ways, he was a fine, loyal friend. 'Twas more than likely we would both die while fighting the Saracens or from wounds inflicted in battle, so his teasing held no substance. Moreover, in my heart, I knew that you deserved a better man than me. If we did survive to return to England, Edric belonged to a high-ranking family, and he would one day inherit his sire's rich estate. He had so much more to offer you than I did."

"Ash!" Oh, God, how could he have believed himself unworthy of her?

"I know you and I had once talked about running away and getting married, but after I committed to going on Crusade, I realized 'twould not be right to bind you to me, when I might be killed. 'Tis why I…let you go. During our journey to the eastern lands, though, especially on the long and lonely nights, I could not help thinking about my life if I did manage to return to England. I missed you so much. I *ached* for you, and—"

A sob welled in her throat. She'd felt the same way about him.

"—and I vowed I would fight for your love. For *our* love. I decided to speak with your father as soon as I got back to Warwickshire. I did not want to live without you, Briar Rose."

Oh, Ash. She wanted to crumple to the stones at his feet and weep, but she must be strong, to hear all that he had to say. Trembling, she asked, "Did you tell Edric of your decision?"

"Not at first. One night, though, a few days into the battle to reclaim Acre, he and some other soldiers had drunk too much. While we sat around the fire, sharing stories, he taunted me. He was relentless. Fed up, I told him that he would never have you, that you loved me and not him, and that I intended to marry you."

"Is that when he wounded you?" Rosetta asked.

"Nay. Not that night. He was furious, and you and I both know he has a strong temper. I half-expected him to start a fight with me, but he did not. He just strode away. The next morning, he seemed to be his usual self. He said no more about what I had told him, and so I thought the disagreement was over. 'Twas one of my mistakes."

"Go on," she urged, dreading what she would hear but needing to know all.

Ash's shoulders tensed. The rigidity of his posture spoke of tremendous inner torment. "Two days later, we were engaged in a skirmish with Saracens. During the battle, Edric and I pursued one particularly brutal enemy warrior who tried to flee. We followed him for some distance, until he turned on us. Together, we fought him. He cut my leg, but I battled through my pain, and Edric and I slew him. As I lowered my weapon, congratulating Edric on our fine fight, he grabbed the fallen Saracen's sword. He turned the weapon on me."

"Oh, God," Rosetta whispered.

"I did not anticipate the attack. He cut my face on his first strike. His eyes glittering with hatred, he said no woman—especially you—would ever find me handsome again. He said you would not be able to bear to look at me."

"Nay," she rasped. "*Nay!*"

"With blood streaming into my eyes, I defended myself, but my injured leg gave out. I fell, unable to stand, and he kicked away my sword. He…slashed my hands, vowing that I would never touch you again, would never be able to…caress you."

Unable to hold back her sobs, Rosetta wept.

"He made sure you would never desire me as your husband."

She pressed her arms over her stomach, tasting bile at the back of her mouth. Edric had deliberately hurt Ash, given him disfiguring scars, because of Ash's love for her. She was responsible for what had happened to him.

"I am sorry," she said, her heart breaking into thousands of tiny, bloody, painful shards. "Oh, God, I am sorry."

Ash touched her shoulder. "'Tis not your fault."

"It is! Oh, Ash—"

He exhaled a ragged breath, and then he pulled her into his arms, holding her head against his chest. His familiar, masculine scent filled her senses, sharpening her anguish, interweaving the present turmoil with memories of their past together. On instinct, her arms went around him, as she'd held him in the past, and she sobbed into his tunic.

He let her cry, whispering soothing words while she wept. After long moments, when she had no more tears to shed, he tipped her face up and placed a tender kiss on her brow.

Shuddering, her eyes stinging, she said, "I am so glad you survived."

A muscle ticked in Ash's jaw. "So am I." He handed her a handkerchief which she used to dry her eyes and nose.

"Tell me the rest. Please."

As she spoke, she sensed him retreating emotionally. She could *not* let him go, not now.

"*Please*. What happened after he wounded you? Did someone else see him attack you, or—?"

"No one else was around, so there were no witnesses. Edric made sure to remind me of that before he threw aside the sword and walked away, leaving me lying on the ground along with the dead Saracen. Edric no doubt hoped that I would bleed to death. If anyone found me, they would believe I had died from wounds inflicted while I fought the enemy warrior. I shouted for help, hoping someone would hear me. I yelled until my voice gave out, until I had lost all hope…and then, some Crusaders found me."

111

"Thank God," she whispered.

"I had lost a lot of blood. I was barely conscious when they pushed me onto a horse and took me first to my superior officers, and then to the Knights Hospitaller. It took me many months to heal, but I vowed I would get well enough to journey back to England."

Frowning, she said, "Did you tell the other Crusaders what happened to you?"

"I tried. I told my friends, and asked them to relay my account to the King. However, Edric denied all, saying he had not wounded me; the Saracen had. It did not help that I soon fell into a fever that lasted for many days. My account of Edric's assault was quickly dismissed as delirium."

"You had no way to prove he was the one responsible," Rosetta murmured. "No proof, as you said earlier."

"Exactly. Even if I had not been feverish, I doubt what I said would have been believed. My wounds, after all, were cut by a foreign weapon. Edric was also an outstanding warrior. He and I were among the first to have been knighted on the battlefield."

Mother Mary. What he had been through was more than anyone should have to endure in a lifetime. "I am sorry about your scars, Ash, so very sorry—"

"Hush," he whispered, kissing her brow again. "You have no reason to apologize."

"I do! Edric attacked you because of me."

Ash shook his head. "Edric is solely to blame for his wickedness. You, Briar Rose, are the reason I am alive."

"Me? But—"

A smile touched his mouth. "The love we shared gave me the will to live. Edric might have damaged me physically, but he could never destroy my love for you. It gave me the strength to heal, and to return to make you mine."

Rosetta trembled in Ash's arms. Ah, God, it felt so *right* to hold her, to be the one she leaned on when she wept. Ash longed to kiss her, to ease some of the remaining torment that must still churn within her, its strength diminished through her weeping but not completely gone.

How curious that his heart felt lighter now that he had told her the truth about his scars. She hadn't tried to pull away from him. She hadn't called him a liar, as he had dreaded. She also hadn't said she did not want to be his—which gave him hope that she'd love him as she had before.

"Our love has given me strength, too," Rosetta said, her words spoken as though she had chosen them with care. "Yet, I do not know how we can be together again."

An icy chill plowed through Ash. "What do you mean? We are together right now. You never have to leave Damsley Keep if you do not want to."

Concern gleamed in her eyes. "I am promised to Edric."

"I do not care."

"My marriage to him was approved by the crown. The banns have already been announced three times in Clipston's church—"

"I will *never* let him wed you."

"Ash—"

"If he was able to wound me without the slightest remorse, what might he dare to do to you?" The iciness within Ash spread to encompass his soul. "I would never forgive myself if he hurt you out of jealousy or anger."

Her lips curved into a sad, shaky smile. Reaching up, she drew her fingertips down his cheek. He closed his eyes, savoring the pleasure of her touch. "As a man of honor," she said softly, "you know the importance of fulfilling a commitment to the crown. 'Tis my *duty* to marry Edric, my duty to my parents as well as to the King."

Ash suppressed a harsh cry of fury. Damnation, but she was right. "There must be a way to break your betrothal, one that would be accepted by your family and the crown."

"I do not know of one." Blinking hard, she looked away into the darkness, as if battling the fresh onslaught of tears.

He caught her free hand and kissed it. "We will find a way."

Her attention returned to him; her gaze glimmered with uncertainty.

"We *will*." He pressed their joined fingers over his heart, where his love for her would always lie, regardless of what happened in the coming days. "No matter how difficult it might be, we must not stop searching until we have figured out what to do."

"Mayhap if we met with my parents, and you told them what you told me tonight—"

"I sent a missive to your father this afternoon," Ash gently pressed her fingers. "I told him that you were safe and my honored guest. I meant to tell you earlier."

Gratitude shone in her eyes, but then her worry returned. "By now, he will know I have been kidnapped. He will bring his men-at-arms to your front gates."

"Aye. I expect him to be here on the morrow."

"Edric will no doubt be with him. Oh, Ash—"

"Neither your father nor Edric will know that I abducted you. Edric will suspect, but will not have any proof."

Fear touched her features. "Do you mean to challenge Edric? Is that why you want my father there, to be a witness?"

She was clever, his Briar Rose: clever and also correct. His first impulse had indeed been to confront Edric and draw him into a deadly fight—something Ash couldn't have done before his wounds had mostly healed and he could once again grip a weapon. "'Tis what I would *like* to do—"

"'Tis too dangerous a plan, especially if he is as good a warrior as you say he is."

"I am a skilled fighter myself."

"Even with the injuries to your hands?"

Her soft inquiry brushed over every thread of doubt in his mind.

"Do you still have the strength in your hands that you had before? I have only held a broadsword once, and 'twas very heavy. I cannot imagine wielding such a weapon, when—"

"I may be disfigured," Ash ground out, "but I am not helpless."

"I did not say that you were." Her stubborn gaze held his. "My concern is that 'twill not be a fair fight."

Ash laughed, the sound bitter. "Briar Rose—"

"—and I *will not* stand by and see you wounded again by Edric…or killed." Her eyes blazed, even as a tear slipped down her cheek.

He stared back, humbled and captivated by the passion in her gaze. That passion came from her feelings for him: from the purest, truest love.

"I must confront Edric," Ash said quietly, wiping away her tear. "He must answer for what he did to me. Moreover, he must accept that you will never be his wife."

"Ash, a duel between you and Edric is not enough to release me from my marriage."

"Even if I kill him?" Ash said with a growl.

"Cease that kind of talk! If you did slay him without proving that he deliberately wounded you, then you would be guilty of murder. There would be no chance of us having a future together then."

Ash squeezed her hand again. "By fighting him, I might be able to prove his dishonor, though—and that might be enough for the crown to reconsider your marriage."

The faintest hope touched her expression. "What do you mean?"

"If I provoke him," Ash continued, "I can make him angry. If he is enraged, he will not be as careful with his words. I might be able to goad him into confessing that he wounded me in the East."

"And if he does not admit to what he did to you?"

Ash shrugged. "Then we are no further ahead than we were before."

"You might be even more badly injured," she said, shaking her head. "Nay, Ash. You cannot undertake such a reckless plan. I will not let you."

Frustration coiled through him. "What do you suggest, then? That I do naught? That I simply stand by and let you leave with your sire and Edric?"

She studied him through the darkness and then nodded.

"*What*?! How in hellfire—?"

Before he guessed her intent, she rose up on tiptoes and kissed him. At the incredible shock of her lithe body gliding against his, followed by the light kiss, the rest of his words vanished.

"The wedding will have to be rescheduled," she said evenly, lowering back down to standing. "That may take several weeks. In the meantime, I can start searching for further proof of Edric's treachery. You said you have some evidence already—"

"I do. However, 'tis not a simple matter to get hold of it." Indeed, the fragile tapestry of contacts and communications he'd established could be ripped asunder if he acted without carefully considering his actions. Informants could die. He did not want good men's deaths on his conscience.

"'Tis why I must do what I can," Rosetta insisted. "After Edric and I became betrothed, I spent more days at Wallensford Keep. If I continue to play the role of his future bride, no one will question my continued visits there. I will even try to go when he is away from the castle."

Ash scowled, fear for her howling within him like a winter gale. "'Tis too risky. I will contact my local informant and try to get a man inside Wallensford—"

"How long will that take to arrange? I can accomplish far more than any stranger to the keep."

"Mayhap so, but if Edric realizes what you are doing, you could be in great peril."

"If I ride to Wallensford Keep when Edric is not there, he cannot hurt me," she said.

"True, but—"

"Edric trusts me. I can go anywhere I want in the castle, including into his private solar."

Ash gritted his teeth. "I like this plan less and less."

"'Tis the best option we have. I can go where you cannot, and I can get into Edric's personal belongings." A hint of cunning in her smile, she added, "I can also find out if he has any more details on the lost treasure. Would that not be helpful? Is that not the kind of information you need as a spy working for the crown?"

Hellfire, what I need is to kiss you. Love you. Make you mine, and spend the rest of my life with you.

"I *want* to do this, Ash," she said, her gaze earnest. "At least give me a chance to see what I can discover."

His arms slid around her waist to hold her tight. "Briar Rose, I cannot—"

"You must. For *us*. I will *not* lose you again."

Her shaking voice, filled with conviction, was his

undoing. With a low groan, he dipped his head and kissed her, his mouth ravenous, seeking.

She answered his kiss with a hungry one of her own. As her lips molded to his, she slipped her hands up the front of his tunic to link them around his neck. Her fingers curled into his hair, the brush of her skin against his nape sending hot-cold sparks shooting down his spine. With each press of his mouth, she answered him with equal fervor. His senses flooded with the unforgettable taste and feel of her.

As their kisses intensified, he pressed her back against the merlon behind her. A gasp broke from her, and then she was kissing him again, her hands moving to claw into the front of his tunic. He suckled her mouth; she nibbled his. He slid his tongue into her mouth; shuddering, she matched the wild dance of his tongue.

"Ash," she panted. "Ash!"

She writhed, as if frantic to get closer to him. As if she wanted to be naked with him.

He crushed his body against hers, his hips flush against hers, his swollen, throbbing hardness pressing against her womanly softness. They groaned together, and he closed his eyes, drowning in desire, his whole body yearning to hike up her skirts and plunge into her.

He could make her his. Right now.

Do it, his mind screamed. *You know 'tis what she wants too.*

Yet, even as his desire roared, he acknowledged the need for discretion. Rosetta was a well-bred lady. A virgin. She deserved to be wooed, loved, and exquisitely pleasured the first time she lay with him—not taken quickly on a chilly, windswept battlement.

"Ash," she moaned against his mouth. As her palm slid down his tunic, on a deliberate path to places he dared not let her touch right now, he caught her wrist.

Breaking the kiss, breathing hard, she stared at him.

"What we want," he whispered, "we cannot finish tonight."

"Because I am a maiden?" Disappointment shone in her eyes.

"Aye." He kissed her, soothing the sting of his refusal. "You are a noble lady—"

"—who sometimes wishes she was not." She sighed and dropped her forehead to the front of his tunic. "Why do you have to be so damned chivalrous?"

He chuckled and kissed the top of her head. "I am a knight. 'Tis my duty—"

She groaned.

"Briar Rose." He nudged his fingers under her chin and eased it up so that she met his gaze. "When we lie together, I want it to be the most special and memorable night of our lives. You deserve a soft bed, sprinkled with wild rose petals, and all of my attention and love. This battlement is neither romantic nor suitable."

Her lips flattened, but then she nodded. With a provocative smile, she said, "For a night as wondrous as you have said, I will wait."

"Good." He kissed her again, a long, thorough kiss filled with promises.

"Will you do one thing for me," she murmured, "when we lie together?"

His lusty mind filled with all kinds of sinful imaginings he would love to explore with her. "What is that?"

"Will you take off your gloves?"

His gust twisted. "God's bones!"

"When you touch me, I want to feel *you*, not leather. I do not care if your hands are scarred. I do not care if they are unpleasant to look upon. Those wounds do not diminish in any way who you are, Ash, especially to me."

He curled his hands on a surge of anguish. She

wouldn't be saying such kind and brave words if she had seen his scars. His hands were hideous. They were grotesque enough to cause nightmares, and thus were best kept hidden. "I will never take off my gloves," he said, drawing away from her. Refusing to acknowledge the dismay in her expression, he said, "Please do not ask me again."

Such finality echoed in Ash's words. Rosetta swallowed hard, hating to think that he'd resolved never to bare his hands again. Surely, the gloves were uncomfortable at times? In the heat of the summer, they must be unbearable.

She studied his profile as he stared down at the bailey below. The night breeze tousled his hair and stirred his garments. That impenetrable, emotional armor seemed to surround him again. Mayhap it would simply take a little more time and trust for him to be willing to take off his gloves. If she loved him, proved to him that his scars really didn't matter to her, he might be less resolute.

Loneliness touched his features, and she moved to his left side and slid her fingers through his. At first, he didn't acknowledge her touch, but then his hand curled around hers.

"I should take you back to your chamber," he said.

"Will you stay with me tonight?"

His narrowed gaze slid to her. "I am tempted. You know I am. Yet, I thought we had agreed to wait, and that we both understood the reasons why."

"I did not mean that we would couple. I meant…that we would lie together, with our clothes on, in each other's arms—as we used to in the meadow near Millenstowe Keep.

Once I return to my father's castle, it might be a while before we can see each other again. It could be days, or even weeks."

He made a rough sound and leaned in to kiss her. "I cannot bear to think about it."

"Neither can I."

As the wind sighed around them, he said softly, "I will stay for a short while. I cannot be with you all night. I will not have the gossips whispering that I seduced another man's betrothed in my bed."

"Even if she is willing to be seduced?" Rosetta asked with a coy smile.

His eyes glinted. "You have wildness in you tonight, Briar Rose."

"Mmm."

Ash chuckled and then freed his hand from hers. He walked with her to the door into the keep.

As they entered the solar, Ash told the guards outside that he and Rosetta were going to talk in private and that no one was to be allowed in. In the quiet chamber, a freshly stoked fire burned in the hearth. Water had been left for Rosetta to wash before bed.

Rosetta slipped off her cloak and laid it next to her circlet and veil on the trestle table, and then took off her shoes. Watching her, Ash pulled off his boots and left them near the door. A thrill chased through her, for so easily she imagined them together in this chamber as lovers, caught up in heated kissing, their garments whispering as they shed them, piece by piece, until they were both naked and tumbling onto the bed.

Struggling to rein in her thoughts, she crossed to the bed. The ropes creaked as she lay down on her back, her head resting on a pillow, her shimmering skirts settling atop the blankets. Ash climbed onto the mattress beside her, and the bed jostled at his weight.

A *thud* sounded from underneath.

Frowning, Ash rolled over and peered under the bed. "Ah. I seem to have found my missing eating knife."

A stinging flush warmed Rosetta's cheeks. She rose, reached under the furnishing, and retrieved the dagger. After brushing off the dust, she handed the sheathed weapon to him. "I was going to tell you—"

He laughed and took the dagger, his gloved fingers closing around it. "Of course you were...months from now."

"Sooner than that." She lay down beside him again on the mattress.

"Were you going to threaten me with the knife? Or mayhap you intended to take poor Herta hostage?"

Rosetta folded her hands across her stomach. "I had not yet decided what I was going to do. My only plan was to use it somehow to escape."

Grinning, Ash turned onto his right side and gazed down at her.

"You are not angry?" She hadn't expected him to be amused.

"If you attacked me, I could easily overpower you."

She rolled her eyes. "How nice to know."

"I do not think, though, that you would ever hurt anyone unless you had to." His expression turned solemn. "Not unless your life or the life of someone you loved was threatened."

"You are right." She truly hoped she never had to face such a situation.

Rising up to sitting, he lifted the hem of his tunic to reveal his shirt underneath. Drawing the dagger, he cut a strip of linen from the garment. "Why did you do that?" she asked, puzzled. "You just ruined your shirt."

"A garment can be replaced." He cut another strip. "You cannot."

"Ash, for God's sake—"

"I am not being foolish," he said firmly. "Our conversation earlier made me realize what I had not before: You are one of the few people in this area to have discovered ancient gold. You are also the only one, I believe, to still be alive."

"What happened to the others?"

"They were murdered."

"Murdered!" she echoed. The thought of such violence made her feel ill.

Ash nodded grimly. "If the wrong people learned of your discovery and wanted to glean from you what you found years ago and where—"

"If you are trying to frighten me, you are succeeding."

Ash slipped the knife back into its sheath. "I do not mean to terrify you. I do, however, want you to be aware of how you are connected to the search for the lost riches. I want you to have a means to defend yourself, especially when you go to Wallensford Keep, because once you leave my castle, I can no longer watch over you. Now, hold out your left arm."

She rolled onto her side facing him and did as he had commanded. Ash pushed up her sleeve as far as it would go, and then tied the knife to her wrist with the strips of linen. "Keep this dagger with you at all times, until you are free to be with me."

A hard edge underscored his words. He had not made a request, but given her an order.

"Promise me, Briar Rose. You will keep this weapon on you or within easy reach. Always. All right?"

His intense concern for her made Rosetta's heart warm with love. "All right."

A sly smile tilted his mouth as he tugged her sleeve back into place, concealing the dagger. He lay back down on his side. "Now that that is settled…you may kiss me."

What an excellent idea, when his mouth was so very close. His crooked grin proved how much he looked forward to the kiss; the wildness inside her coaxed her to make him work for it.

Propped up on one arm, she raised her brows. "I *may* kiss you? As in you have granted me your lordly permission?"

"Aye." Mischief danced in his eyes.

She giggled, and her gaze settled on his lips. "What kind of a kiss, though? A quick pressing together of our lips? Or a lusty clashing of our mouths and tongues?"

"Since I am endeavoring to be honorable tonight, I suggest a quick kiss."

"I knew you would." She leaned in and pressed her lips to his, delighted when his mouth opened beneath hers to tease, tempt, and seduce. He kissed her with such pure love, such shattering honesty, she was glad when the kiss didn't turn out to be at all quick.

At last, the rhythm of their kisses slowed, gentled. He lay back and drew her over to him, so that her head rested on his chest and her right arm lay across his belly. She closed her eyes, savoring his warmth and the moment of contentment.

"I am glad you returned to England," she said softly.

He chuckled. "Even though I kidnapped you?"

"Even though you kidnapped me."

She sighed, feeling blissfully sleepy. If only she could stay with Ash like this forever.

Even as she dared to indulge in such a dream, a dark thread of foreboding wound around her heart.

"That was a silly move, Uncle."

Perched on the end of Justin's bed, with the chamber illuminated by several flickering candles, Ash studied the chess board lying between him and the boy. The lad had suffered another upsetting dream about his father. After Ash had sat with him for a long while and comforted him, Justin had asked for a game of chess.

'Twas the middle of the night, but if a game of chess would help Justin get back to sleep then they would play a game of chess. Justin had chosen the black pieces, leaving Ash to use the white ones.

"Uncle—"

"Sorry." Ash's gaze traveled over the wood and leather board inlaid with silver; the pieces were carved from bone. He'd found the set in a shop in London while waiting to meet with a fellow spy. "Ah. I see my mistake now. You can take my queen."

Justin frowned. "Are you sleeping with your eyes open?"

Ash laughed. "Nay, I am awake." His thoughts, though, were not on the game, but with Rosetta in the solar. It had been difficult leaving her. Kissing her tonight, lying with her curled up next to him, had only reinforced to him just how much he wanted her to be his wife. Having her by his side, each and every day, would make his life complete.

To think of her searching for damning information on Edric… He hated the thought of her putting herself in such peril. One simple mistake—as he'd made by moving his pawn moments ago without paying too much heed to the other pieces on the board—and their lives could be forever changed.

"If you like, you can move back your knight," Justin said. "I will pretend I did not notice."

"'Tis most chivalrous of you," Ash said with a rueful smile, "but I will accept my error in judgment. I will be more careful with my next move."

Justin moved his bishop to take Ash's queen and then removed the piece from the board.

Rubbing his thumb over the carving of a woman wearing long robes and a crown, Justin asked, "Do you think Lady Montgomery knows how to play chess?"

"She does. I taught her."

"When? In the last couple of days?"

Ash shook his head. "She and I used to play years ago, when I was but a squire at her father's castle."

"You knew her *that* long ago?"

The lad made "*that* long ago" sound like an eternity. In some ways, though, it had been. "Once, I even thought of marrying Rosetta." Ash pushed a pawn forward two spaces on the board.

Justin stared at him.

"Your move," Ash said, gesturing to the chess pieces.

"I know, Uncle, but… Why did you not marry her?"

"I went on Crusade. I did not think it fair—"

"You are back in Warwickshire now. There is no reason why you cannot ask her to be your wife."

The lad's voice held such enthusiasm. Did Justin like to think of Rosetta living permanently at Damsley Keep and always being around to help him with his archery practice? "'Tis not so simple," Ash said. "There are other circumstances and people to consider."

"The man who gave her that ring, you mean?" Justin snorted. "'Tis an ugly jewel. She deserves something beautiful."

Ash chuckled; he simply couldn't help it, for he hated the ring too. "Aye, well—"

"Do you love Lady Montgomery, Uncle?"

The startling question snatched the air from Ash's lungs. He looked over at his own bed, the sheets rumpled and empty. Never had he imagined that a question would make him feel like he'd been punched hard in the gut.

"Well, do you?"

He sighed. "I do. Very much."

Justin grinned. Swapping the white queen to his left hand, the boy ran his finger over the points of the piece's crown. "In the old tales you have told me, the knight never gives up on his quest. 'Tis his duty to do what is right, and to fight for what he believes in, is it not?"

A sense of disquiet rippled through Ash. "True."

"You are a knight, aye?"

"You know that I am."

Justin studied him most solemnly, while candlelight played over wall beside him. "If you love her, Uncle, you must fight for her. You must win her away from that other man."

"Do not worry. I intend to."

"Promise?"

The boy was most serious. "I promise," Ash said. He held Justin's gaze; they'd talked before about the importance of a solemn oath.

The lad smiled as if he had just won the game. Handing the queen to Ash, he said, "I am weary of chess. Can we finish our game tomorrow?"

Chapter Twelve

Rosetta smothered a yawn with her hand as she strolled along the path meandering through the beds of roses. Dew winked on the fragrant blooms, and the clear sky promised another bright, sunny day, but her head felt muzzy and her heart unsettled.

Ash hadn't stayed long in the solar last night, and so she had gone to bed, putting the knife he'd given her on the bedside table. She had also taken off her ring. She would have to wear it again in the morning, in case her father and Edric arrived at Damsley Keep, but while she slept in Ash's bed and longed for him to be with her, kissing her, loving her, she'd savor being free of the jewel's weight on her finger.

As the night had worn on, and the blaze in the hearth had burned down to glowing embers, her restless thoughts had refused to settle. She'd lain awake staring at the dwindling play of firelight on the shadowed walls and imagining how her life might have been if Ash had never gone on Crusade with Edric.

After rising early and tying the dagger to her left wrist as Ash had done, Rosetta had donned her garments and ring and asked for a walk so she could enjoy some fresh morning air. Herta had brought her to the garden. Wandering through the beautiful roses—some of the blooms were larger than her hand—was already helping to lighten her mood.

The crunch of stones sounded behind her on the path, and excitement made her pulse quicken. Had Ash come to see her? She quickly turned, her fingers brushing a blood-red rose that was ready to drop its petals. Justin strode toward her, carrying his bow, his quiver slung over his shoulder. The boy appeared as unkempt as ever, but seemed happier than he'd been yesterday.

"Good day, milady."

"Good day to you, Justin."

"Herta told me you were in the garden."

Gesturing to the bow, Rosetta asked, "Are you on your way to practice your archery?"

"Nay, milady. I thought I would see if you are ready for another session."

Astonishment flitted through her, but she pretended to be distracted by a bird darting through the rose bushes.

"You seemed to enjoy yesterday's lesson, so I thought we should continue today." The boy hesitated. "You *do* still want to know how to use a bow and arrows, in case you are trapped in a siege, do you not?"

"I most certainly do."

"I thought so." Justin's freckled face lit with a grin. "Yesterday, I told my uncle that I was teaching you. He did not seem to mind."

"I am glad." Indeed, she was most relieved. Justin had seemed quite concerned that he didn't fail the man, whoever he was. She also didn't want the boy to be punished for being in the garden with her, when he might be expected to complete chores or other duties elsewhere. She had already resolved that if the boy got into trouble, she would speak to the uncle on the lad's behalf.

His eyes sparkling, Justin said, "Uncle even said he

was proud of me."

Rosetta smiled. "I am, too. After all, your quest—to teach me how to use the weapon—is very noble."

The lad nodded. A secretive smile touched his lips, as if he was thinking back to a recent situation or conversation, mayhap one involving his uncle. Then he scratched his head, causing his hair to be even more untidy. "Before we start, I was wondering… Do you like puppies?"

"Of course. Do you?"

"Aye. Would you like to see the one that I am going to have? 'Tis not old enough to leave its mother yet, but will be in a few sennights."

"I would love to."

"Follow me then." He turned on his heel and marched off toward the garden gate. She smothered a laugh, because in that moment, for some reason, he reminded her of a younger Ash. A foolish thought, though, for Ash didn't have children; he would have told her if he had.

Ever gallant, Justin held the gate for her as she stepped through, and he led her to the stable. The grooms seemed surprised to see her, but bowed respectfully as she passed by them and went with the boy to the end stall.

"Oh, look at them!" Rosetta whispered, kneeling beside Justin on the straw. The puppies made the most adorable whimpering sounds as they suckled their mother.

Justin set aside his bow and quiver. "This one is mine," he said, pointing to the smallest one.

"Is it a he or a she?" Rosetta asked.

Justin frowned. "A boy, I think. I am not certain, though. I will look and see if it has a—"

"Do not bother it right now," Rosetta said quickly, "since 'tis busy eating." Mercy, but she didn't want to be drawn into an awkward discussion about the difference between boy and girl puppies.

"All right." The boy smiled up at her. "Do you like

the one I chose?"

"I do. It has very nice coloring."

A metallic groaning noise carried from outside: the sound of the portcullis rising. Men's voices also drifted in from the bailey.

Rosetta curled her hand into the prickly straw. Had her father and Edric come to collect her? Last night, Ash had said her sire would likely arrive today. Part of her longed to jump up and run to the doorway of the stable to see what was happening. Another part of her was reluctant to have to leave the castle and be separated from Ash.

Drawing in a steadying breath, she decided to stay with Justin. Her sire and Edric might not have arrived; the portcullis could have been raised to let in a merchant delivering goods. If her sire *had* come for her, Ash would find her.

"My puppy is lucky," Justin said, shifting on his knees beside her.

"Why is that?" she asked, noting the sudden sadness in the boy's expression.

"It has a mother." He toyed with a bit of straw. "My mother is dead."

"I am sorry to hear that," Rosetta murmured.

"She died when I was little. My father is dead, too. He passed on over a month ago."

Tears pricked Rosetta's eyes. She couldn't imagine being so young and having lost both parents. That must be why the uncle had taken Justin into his care. She slid her arm around the boy's shoulders, noting how scrawny he seemed beneath his tunic.

"Do you have a mother and a father?" he asked, peering up at her.

"I do. They live in a castle not far from Damsley Keep."

Justin swallowed hard. His voice wavering, he said, "I

miss my parents."

"I am sure you do," she said gently.

"I have nightmares. Sometimes, I am so afraid of having a bad dream that I cannot sleep. My uncle stays in my room at night now, in case I get frightened."

This poor boy had endured so much. Rosetta drew him in closer, and without hesitation, he rested his head on her shoulder. Over his sniffles, she said, "I vow that your mother and father are watching over you every day."

"Really? How do you know?" Justin wiped his eyes.

"I just do." She hugged him tighter. "Ladies know such things."

Justin chuckled and then sniffled again. "What about knights?"

"Some of them, I am sure, know such things too."

"What about my uncle? Does he know that my parents are watching over me?"

"I expect he does. 'Tis why he is taking extra special care of you. Your parents are no doubt very proud of both him and you."

"Milord."

Standing near the chopping block in the kitchens, Ash glanced up from where he'd been consulting with the cook about dried beans, lentils, spices, almonds, and other foods that needed to be restocked in the keep's pantry—a mundane task that had kept his mind somewhat distracted. From the moment he had woken, he hadn't been able to ward off the acute sense of unease that had rooted within him, a feeling that something life-changing and important was about to happen. When he saw the armed guard standing in the kitchen doorway, Ash knew the moment of reckoning was upon him.

"Riders at the gates?" Ash asked.

"Lords Montgomery and Sherborne, milord. You asked to be informed immediately if they arrived."

"So I did." Ash marveled at the steadiness of his voice; a ghastly coldness had gripped his innards. He was about to lose Rosetta. Again. He'd sacrifice his very soul to keep her at Damsley Keep, but she'd been right that she might be able to find information at Wallensford Keep that would incriminate Edric. How damned ironic that to earn the chance to love her forever, Ash had to let her go.

"Raise the portcullis and let our guests in," Ash said to the guard. "I will be there in a moment." As the man headed back to his post, Ash turned to the cook. "We will finish our discussion another day."

The plump woman curtsied, stowed the parchment on a shelf, and headed off to check on the pottage bubbling in large pots hung over the cooking fires.

Ash strode out into the bright sunlight and headed for the garden. Herta had told him that Rosetta had requested a morning walk, and she might still be strolling along the paths.

Amongst the women drawing water from the well, he spied Herta. Crossing to her, he said, "Lady Montgomery. Is she still in the garden?"

The young woman shook her head. "My betrothed just told me that she is in the stable."

Ash frowned. "Why did she go there?"

"Justin was with her. I think he wanted to show her the puppies."

"Ah. Thank you." Ash went to the stables. When he entered the shadowed building, he recognized Rosetta's voice, hushed as though she was offering comfort. He softened his strides, muffling the crackle of straw beneath his boots. Justin spoke next, his words indistinct, but the wobble in his voice was clear. He was upset.

Ash forced down a dismayed sigh. He had tried every means he could think of to help ease the boy's grief, and yet, it seemed as if Ash's efforts hadn't made one whit of difference. He couldn't blame Justin for wanting to confide in someone else.

Ash neared the doorway to the stable where the wolfhound and her pups lay. He halted and peered in, and his breath froze in his chest. Rosetta knelt with her arm around Justin, her fine gown and cloak pooling on the straw. The lad, pressed against her, seemed to be soaking in her tender words.

They looked as if they could be mother and son.

A molten rush of pride and longing filled Ash. He didn't move from the doorway, for he didn't want to interrupt the poignant moment. If he had run away with Rosetta and married her years ago, he'd have seen her like this often, comforting their children.

"What about my uncle?" Justin was saying. "Does he know that my parents are watching over me?"

Rosetta smiled, her lovely features softened with compassion. "I expect he does. 'Tis why he is taking extra special care of you. Your parents are no doubt very proud of both him and you."

Ah, God. Tears burned Ash's eyes. He didn't want to let her go. If there was any way of stopping her from leaving...

He must have made some small sound, for Rosetta glanced over her shoulder and saw him. Uncertainty flickered across her features as she loosened her hold on Justin.

"Look who has found us," she said.

Scrubbing at his eyes with a grubby hand, Justin glanced at Ash. The boy's face reddened, as though he was embarrassed to have been caught crying. "Uncle."

"Uncle?" Rosetta sounded shocked.

Ash nodded. "I am Justin's guardian. He is my late brother's son."

Brushing off her cloak, she rose. "I…did not realize."

As Ash met her gaze, he longed to answer the questions he saw in her eyes, but that conversation would have to wait; there were more pressing matters now. "I am sorry to have had to interrupt," Ash said to her, "but Edric and your sire are here."

Grumbling, Justin picked up his bow and arrows. "Are the visitors important? I was going to help Lady Montgomery use the bow again this morning."

"I am afraid that will not be possible," Ash said gently. "Her ladyship will be leaving us."

Justin's face crumpled with dismay. "Nay! Why?"

"Her father and betrothed have come to take her home."

The boy frowned, and then resolve touched his gaze. "But, I thought… Last night, Uncle, when we talked—"

"We will discuss that later. Come," Ash said. "They are waiting." He escorted Rosetta and Justin back through the stable to the bailey.

A short distance inside the gatehouse, two riders had halted, along with their escort of six armed guards. A stocky, broad-shouldered man with gray hair sat astride a chestnut destrier: Rosetta's father. Next to him, on a dappled gray, was a younger lord with shoulder-length, light brown hair: *Edric.*

The bastard looked exactly as he had done months ago, the last time Ash had seen him. Fighting for consciousness, lying on a stretcher and due to be taken to the Knights Hospitaller, Ash had looked at Edric and told his superiors that Edric was the man who had cut his face and hands—not the Saracen they had slain. Edric, without the slightest trace of guilt, had denied all, and the others had believed him. The whoreson had even had the gall to tuck the blanket more closely around Ash.

Hot, blistering rage had boiled within Ash then, as it did now. He'd vowed never to speak to Edric again; regrettably, he might have to break that vow today.

"Rosetta!" Edric dismounted and hurried to her.

Ash met Edric's gaze for the barest moment—a lethal glare that would have quelled most men—and then pointedly snapped his gaze away. He continued walking toward Rosetta's father, Justin close behind him.

"Lord Montgomery." Ash bowed to Rosetta's sire, who had also dismounted. Ash hadn't lived at Millenstowe Keep for many years now, but he still felt in awe of the great man he had once served.

"Ash." Rosetta's father bowed in return. As he straightened, his attention shifted to Ash's scar. He swiftly looked away, but not before Ash had seen the regret in his lordship's eyes that were the same blue as Rosetta's.

"I realize I look a little different than the last time you saw me," Ash said. "I have several permanent reminders of my days on Crusade."

"Marks of honor, then."

Rosetta had said the same thing, but there was no honor in wounds delivered by a fellow soldier who had once been a best friend. However, Ash chose not to correct his lordship; there would be a better moment for such a discussion.

"Is this your son?" Lord Montgomery asked, gesturing to Justin, who stood holding his bow.

"This is my nephew, Justin. I do not have any children of my own."

"Ah," his lordship said. "I thought mayhap you had married in the past few years and I was unaware of your nuptials."

"Nay, milord." *No other woman could ever compare to Rosetta. She is the only one I want to be my wife.*

Lord Montgomery smiled at the boy. "Good day to you, Justin."

"Good day." The lad executed an awkward bow that almost had him falling face first on the ground. Ash would have to help Justin master the art of the courtly bow.

Footfalls approached, and Ash's shoulders instinctively tensed. Edric was drawing near. Ash balled his hands into fists and struggled to control his fury. How he longed to lunge at Edric, wrestle him down to the dirt, and pummel him until he bloody well admitted what he'd done that day in the East.

Such an attack in front of witnesses, though—as Rosetta had warned him—might not coerce Edric into confessing. Since only Rosetta knew the truth of Ash's scars, the others might think Ash's attack was unprovoked and rush to Edric's rescue. The last thing Ash wanted was to give the conniving bastard an opportunity to earn undeserved sympathy, especially from Rosetta's father.

Nay. For Ash's magnificent Briar Rose, for the love they fought to keep, he must be patient and do as they had agreed last night.

Ah, God, but he could not *wait* for Edric to leave.

"Ash." Edric halted a few paces away, his arm around Rosetta's waist. "'Tis good to see you again."

You ruthless, lying whoreson. Ash's rage flared at the sight of Edric touching Rosetta, but he forced the emotion back down. "There has been much to do in the weeks since I returned to England. Otherwise, I might have paid you a visit."

Wariness flickered in Edric's eyes, before it vanished and his gaze dropped to Justin. "Did you say this lad is your nephew?"

"He is. When my brother died, the crown appointed me Justin's guardian."

"You are not just a lord, then, but a father."

"I do not regret being either."

Ash sensed Rosetta's gaze upon him. He glanced at her, acknowledging the compassion in her expression, and then looked back at her father. Dark smudges under his lordship's eyes indicated he had spent sleepless nights worrying about his beloved daughter. Ash suppressed a pang of guilt; once he had explained all to Lord Montgomery in private, he hoped the man would understand the reasons for Ash's actions.

"I am curious as to how Rosetta came to be at your castle." Edric's tone was pleasant enough, but Ash caught the animosity weaving through the words. "Would you care to explain?"

Not to you, you bastard.

"There were reports of a rider on a black steed in Clipston," Lord Montgomery said. "He was wearing a helm to conceal his face. We believe Rosetta was kidnapped by that man."

"Indeed I was, Father."

Ash's heart jolted. He hadn't expected Rosetta to answer, especially in that manner. Surely she wasn't going to betray him to her sire and Edric? He glanced at her, but her expression remained calm. *Trust her*, his conscience urged. *Whatever she intends, you know she loves you and will never forsake you.*

"Do you own a black horse, Ash?" Edric asked.

Smug triumph warmed Ash's gut. "I do."

Edric's lip curled. "I knew it."

"You knew that I owned a black steed?" Ash asked politely. "How clever of you, since to my knowledge, you have never seen my horses."

His face reddening with anger, Edric dropped his arm from Rosetta's waist. "You abducted Rosetta. You stopped our wedding."

Ash clenched his fists so hard, pain shot through his

fingers. He couldn't wait to see Edric's face when he admitted he *had* stopped the nuptials. Ash drew in a harsh breath, the force of his rage tempting him to admit to the truth right here, right now, regardless of the consequences. "Indeed, I—

"Enough," Rosetta cut in sharply. "Ash did not abduct me."

Astonishment shocked some of the fury from Ash's veins.

"You were right about me being abducted," Rosetta said, her expression unyielding as she stared at Ash, then Edric, and then her father. "The horseman—whoever he was; I never saw his face—pursued me into an alley. During my attempt to escape him, I fell off my mare; 'tis why my gown and cloak are stained. I hit my head and was rendered unconscious—"

"God's blood!" Lord Montgomery said, clearly appalled.

"—so the rider put me on his horse and rode off. I woke some moments later to find myself in his arms. I struggled, managed to break free, and ran into the nearby woods, where I hid. The rider searched for me, but not long after, Ash rode by. You told me you had gone to Clipston, Ash, but the shop you intended to visit was closed because of the wedding?"

Before Ash could say one word, she continued: "What matters is that I recognized Ash and ran out of the trees to him. He was surprised to see me, but then the rider emerged from the forest. To protect me, Ash drew his sword and challenged the lout, who fought Ash but quickly realized Ash was a far superior opponent. The horseman fled, and Ash helped me onto his destrier and brought me to Damsley Keep. I have been a guest here ever since." She beamed at Ash. "I cannot thank him enough for tending to my wounds and for his kindness."

"She stayed in Uncle's solar," Justin said. "She got to sleep in the best bed in the keep."

"The *solar*?" Edric choked out.

"So I did," Rosetta said. "Ash was very gracious to give up his chamber for me."

Anger and suspicion shadowed Edric's expression. "What you just told us, Rosetta... 'Tis what really happened?"

"Aye."

"Are you certain you do not know who kidnapped you?"

She shuddered and hugged herself, and Ash's admiration for her deepened, for she was so convincing, he might believe her himself if he didn't know better. "I did not see his face. He never took off his helm. By now, he has probably destroyed it. We may never know his identity."

"I am very glad you are all right, Daughter, thanks to Lord Blakeley's timely intervention. Yet, who would have reason to abduct you?" Lord Montgomery frowned. "Did the rider say what he wanted? Was he planning to hold you for ransom? Or was he intending to make some other kind of demand from me or Edric?"

"I am sorry, Father. He did not reveal to me what he wanted."

I wanted you, Briar Rose. As I still want you. I will yearn for you until at last, we are together again, this time forever.

"Well." Edric sighed and set his hand on his sword's grip. "'Tis most disappointing that after days of searching and investigating, we are no closer to knowing who the knave is or why he went after Rosetta."

She touched his shoulder. "At least no one was badly hurt or killed. Truth be told, I am eager to return to Millenstowe Keep and set a new date for our wedding."

Edric's gaze warmed with affection. "I want that too, my love."

She is not yours, Edric. She never will be! Bile seared the back of Ash's mouth. How he wanted to smash his fist into Edric's face—

"Are you all right, Ash?" From Lord Montgomery's puzzled expression, he had noticed but didn't understand the animosity between Ash and Edric. Of course, the last time he had seen them, the day they'd left for Crusade, they had been the closest of friends.

"I am fine, milord." Ash did his best to seem disgruntled. "I am as disappointed as Edric, though, that the man responsible has not been captured. I wish there was some way I could help."

"You have been a great help already," Rosetta said, gazing up at him. Love for her overtook Ash's anger and he couldn't hold back a smile.

"We owe you our deepest gratitude, Ash," Lord Montgomery said. "I am sure that if we persevere in our efforts to track down the kidnapper, we will find him." He crossed to Rosetta and embraced her in a fatherly hug. "Meanwhile, we will get you home to Millenstowe Keep. Your mother is anxious to see you and know that you are all right. Edric and his men will escort you, for I have an errand to run before returning home." As he drew back, holding Rosetta at arm's length, he said, "Try to get some rest. You have been through quite an ordeal over the past few days."

"Indeed you have, my love," Edric said.

Rosetta nodded. "I will, Father."

"Ash, if you hear any news that might be relevant to our search, you will notify me or Edric right away?" Lord Montgomery asked, taking the reins of his destrier from one of his men-at-arms.

"I will be sure to notify you, milord."

"Rosetta," Edric said, "you will ride with me."

"All right. I will be there in a moment."

Edric appeared hesitant to let Rosetta leave his side,

but he strode to his mount. She turned to Justin, crouched, and hugged him. "I cannot wait to hear how you are coming along with your archery."

Justin pouted as he tightly hugged her back. "Do you have to go?"

"I am afraid I do."

"I will miss you, Lady Montgomery."

"I will miss you, too. And please, call me Rosetta. We are close friends now, after all." She tousled the lad's hair as she straightened, and then looked up at Ash. His heart ached, as keenly as it had when he had left her years ago. She rose on tiptoes and swiftly embraced him. "I will see you soon," she whispered against his ear.

"Be careful," he whispered back. As she eased away from him, he said, "If by chance you have left any items in the solar—"

"My circlet and veil. Hairpins." Rosetta's lips quivered, as if she was determined to smile despite her welling tears. "Who knows what trouble I might get into with those hairpins?"

I do. He smiled back. "I will send the items on to Millenstowe Keep."

"Thank you."

He stood by as Edric helped Rosetta onto the gray horse and then rose into the saddle behind her. Bitterness and jealousy ripped through Ash at the sight of her sitting between Edric's thighs. Every moment of the ride, Edric would be aware of her luscious body jostling against his.

Damn him!

"Good day, Ash," Edric called. Grabbing hold of his mount's reins, he wheeled the animal around and headed back through the gatehouse to the drawbridge that led out onto the open road. Four men-at-arms fell in behind him.

"Until we meet again, Ash," Lord Montgomery said. As their gazes met, his lordship nodded, the slightest dip of his head. Ash discreetly nodded back.

The private meeting he'd requested with Lord Montgomery for later that morning was on.

Rosetta kept her gaze on the weed-strewn dirt road ahead. She didn't dare glance back across the drawbridge to see Ash one last time, or the tears she was trying her hardest to hold back would spill forth. How she hoped that she could return to Ash soon. And Justin. She'd grown very fond of the boy.

With each gritty clop of the horse's hooves, she swayed against Edric. He held his mount's reins in his right hand, while his left arm curled around her waist, holding her against him. His broad legs were alongside hers, trapping her cloak and gown beneath them and further confining her.

No doubt he wasn't trying to confine her at all; he was simply supporting her while she rode the big, headstrong, unfamiliar horse. And yet, his hold left her ice cold inside. She hadn't known about Edric's terrible attack on Ash before; now, she didn't want to be close to Edric or alone with him.

You must endure, though. Just a little while longer, until you have the proof you need.

Edric leaned in, the rough stubble of his jaw grazing her cheek. "What are you thinking, my love?"

Do not make him suspicious. Convince him you are still willing to be his bride. "I am relieved to be going home. I am also enjoying the pleasant ride and being close to you."

He chuckled, clearly delighted by her words. "Are you comfortable enough?"

"I am. Thank you."

Edric pulled his arm in a little tighter so it rested under her breasts.

Frowning, she reached up and pushed his arm down.

Edric chuckled.

"You were rather brazen just then, Lord Sherborne," she said, forcing lightness into her tone.

"Forgive me if I offended you, but I cannot help my boldness. We were to be husband and wife by now." He kissed her cheek. "I have missed you so much. I have not been able to eat, sleep, or rest, and was nigh frantic when I thought that we might not find you—"

"But in the end, you did."

Edric's rough exhalation stirred her hair. "I will find the man who abducted you. When I do, I will exact a written confession from him. Then I will run him through with my sword."

She shivered at his menacing words. "There is no need for such violence, Edric."

"He kidnapped you—my innocent betrothed—on my lands. As lord, I have a right to demand justice. Such villainy must not go unpunished, my love."

This merciless man didn't sound like the Edric she knew. Rosetta swiveled to glance at him, ignoring the binding tightness of silk that was close to tearing. "I do not want any man to die for what happened in Clipston."

Edric's gaze sharpened. "You sound as if you wish to protect the bastard."

"I do not like bloodshed. I especially do not want a man to lose his life because of me."

"You always were a kind, forgiving soul." As she faced forward again, Edric nuzzled the back of her hair. "'Tis one of the reasons why I love you."

Oh, mercy, but she *didn't* love him. All of her love belonged to Ash.

"I was going to wait a little longer to tell you," Edric

murmured, "but I have a surprise for you."

"A surprise?" she echoed.

"We are not going straight to Millenstowe Keep."

Shock jarred through her, and she covered her reaction by adjusting the ring on her finger. "Oh? Where are we going?"

"To the church in Clipston."

"The church—?"

"Aye, my love. We are to be married as soon as possible."

Chapter Thirteen

anic sluiced through Rosetta, as numbing as if she'd fallen into a frozen river. "Married? Today?"

"I have booked the finest room at Clipston's tavern," Edric said. "Once we are wed, we will go there and…celebrate."

Oh, God. Oh, God!

"Edric, we cannot wed today."

He kissed her cheek again. "Why not? The banns have been announced on three consecutive Sundays, as is required by law. All we need is the priest to conduct the ceremony."

Rosetta's frantic mind raced. She had to stop this reckless plan. She was *not* going to marry Edric, not under any circumstances. "We were going to set a new date, remember? My parents will want to be at the ceremony, and so will all of the friends we invited before."

"If it means so much to you to have them witness our marriage—"

"It does!"

"Then we will have a special celebration in a sennight or so. We will invite everyone to join us at Wallensford Keep for the feast, dancing, and merriment we had to postpone because you were abducted."

"Edric," Rosetta said firmly, swiveling again to meet his gaze.

"I have been very patient." His lustful gaze dropped to her lips. "I see no reason for us to wait, when we are in love."

Oh, dear God. How did she tell him that she didn't love him after all, and that the wedding was off? She needed to be careful, but she also didn't want to end up married to him. She was simply going to have to tell him the truth. "I cannot marry you, Edric. I am sorry."

His expression hardened. Confusion now shadowed his gaze. "What do you mean?"

"I mean…that I have changed my mind."

He drew the horse to an abrupt halt. The animal flailed its head, and its mane whipped into her face. As she pressed her palm to her stinging skin, Edric brought the horse under control. The men-at-arms, now riding two in front and two in behind, also halted their mounts. "You refuse to marry me?" Edric shouted, his words carrying across the nearby fields.

Fear shivered through her; it became even more excruciating when she saw the torment in his eyes. "I…I do not care for you…as I should."

His face went ashen. Then, an ugly redness suffused his features. "'Tis because of Ash," he snarled. "He rescued you, seduced you—"

"He did *not* seduce me!"

"Do not speak to me as if I am a fool!"

"I did not think I had." She frowned. "I regret that you are so upset, but I cannot—"

"Cannot?" He laughed harshly. "I see I made a mistake in giving you a choice." He signaled his men-at-arms to continue and spurred the horse to a brisk walk.

The chill inside her settled into her bones. "What are

you doing? I just told you—"

"I do not care what you just told me."

Anger melted some of her numbness and turned it into seething fury. "Stop this horse. Right now."

"Rosetta," he said. "Be reasonable."

"I am. Stop this horse."

"You do realize it does not matter whether you love me or not? The crown approved our union. That consent is binding."

"I will *not* marry you. Not after what you did to Ash."

As soon as the words left her mouth, she froze. *Oh, God.* She shouldn't have admitted she knew what Edric had done.

"What I did to Ash?" Edric chortled, a sound of disgust. "Did he tell you that false tale about how I cut him with a Saracen sword and left him to die?"

Rosetta shuddered. "Ash does not lie."

"He would tell you whatever he thought you needed to hear, my love, in order to win you away from me."

Unease sifted through her, but she mentally forced it aside. She loved Ash. Without question, she believed what he had told her about his scars and Edric's treachery.

"Ash always resented that he had to part ways with you in order to go on Crusade. His discontent remained with him every day of our travels."

He and I will *marry,* Rosetta's heart cried. *He loves me, as deeply as I love him.*

"You have grown into a beautiful woman, Rosetta," Edric continued, "a worthy prize for any lord. Moreover, Ash realizes that whoever marries you will be able to claim your father's estate when your sire dies. Ash wants those fine lands of your father's for himself."

"Nay," she whispered. "Ash would never—"

"Never?" Edric laughed. "How little you really know of him."

Desperation and anger made her gasp in outrage. "I will not sit here and listen to any more of your wickedness. I will ask you one more time: Stop this horse."

When he made no move to do so, she grabbed for the reins, but he yanked her back with the arm around her waist. "As I told you before, Rosetta, we are going to Clipston."

"You might be. I am going back to Damsley Keep."

Edric laughed as though she'd told him a hilarious jest. She dug her fingernails into his wrist, trying to loosen his hold on her, while she kicked back with her legs.

"Quit struggling. You are going to get hurt," Edric warned.

"I will fight my way off this horse!"

"Do not be foolish. I know of men who have died after falling from their destriers."

"Let me go, then—or I will do whatever it takes to get down from his beast."

Edric snapped a command to his men-at-arms. They fell in alongside his mount, two on either side, effectively blocking her in. When she struggled again, Edric slid his hand up to crush her throat. "Protest all you like, my love. 'Twill not change what happens between us this day."

"Bastard," she choked out.

"I can be, if you refuse to do as I say. I can order these men to return to Damsley Keep and slay Ash and his young charge. Is that what you want?"

Her fear became a hard fist digging fingers into her ribcage. "Your men will never get through the gates," she said, struggling to breathe.

"They will say they have a message from you, one that must be delivered to Ash and Justin in private." Edric's laughter, full of glee, made her tremble. "Do *you* think Ash will order his men to raise the portcullis?"

Ash squatted beside his linen chests that had been returned to the solar and shoved aside garments to retrieve the rolled parchments. He pulled out the one with the drawing of the gold ring Rosetta had found. The sketch by itself was not much proof of a lost treasure. Yet, Ash had decided to share with Lord Montgomery the news of the other two finds Niles had mentioned, as well as where Rosetta had discovered the ancient jewel. Together, the information might be enough to convince Lord Montgomery of the very real danger the hoard posed—a danger that affected every lord within several leagues of the gold finds as well as King Richard's hold on the throne.

A troubled sigh came from behind Ash. He glanced over his shoulder to see Justin sitting on the end of the bed, which had not yet been stripped and remade with clean linens. The boy sat with one arm propped on his right knee, his chin in his palm. His bow and quiver lay on the planks by his feet. "I miss Rosetta," Justin said.

"So do I," Ash murmured. Memories of her lingered in the room. By the hearth, they'd shared their first meal after years apart. Against the wall to his right, after she'd thrown wine in his face, they'd kissed again. On the bed, just last night, they'd lain in each other's arms and burned to consummate their love. Despite how much they cared for one another, he'd had to let her go—and he damned well hated it.

"I do not like Edric."

"Nor do I," Ash agreed, "but—"

"He seemed full of anger." Justin frowned. "I hope he will not harm Rosetta."

Such thoughts tormented Ash too, but in truth, Edric would be unwise to hurt her in any way and risk offending her sire, especially when the wedding had yet to be rescheduled. Also, Edric genuinely cared about Rosetta. He'd cherished her friendship growing up, and he had loved her enough to ask her to be his wife, when as a hero of the Crusades, he could have asked the crown for any noblewoman he wanted—such as a wealthy, young widow with her own lands. Edric must truly love Rosetta, to have waited for her as he had...

Unless he had another, far less noble reason for wanting to marry her.

Ash's focus shifted to the parchment. A sickening chill tore through him as his hand closed around the drawing. If Edric knew about the treasure—

"Why did you let Rosetta go with him? We talked last night about the old stories and the duties of knights."

"Mmm?" Ash's grip tightened on the parchment. If Edric wanted to claim the ancient gold...

"You promised to fight for Rosetta, Uncle. You promised to protect her."

"Justin—"

"Why did you not stop Edric from taking her away?"

Ash dragged his free hand through his hair. He couldn't tell Justin that Rosetta had chosen to leave, or the reasons why; the boy simply wouldn't understand the complexity of the situation, and he might get upset.

And yet... If Ash shared all of his suspicions with Lord Montgomery, including Edric's connection to traitors plotting to overthrow the King, his lordship would most likely agree that the marriage should never go ahead.

Ash snatched up the other relevant parchments and pushed to his feet, anticipation spreading through him like wildfire.

"I thought you loved Rosetta," Justin said. "You told

me you did."

Crossing to the boy, Ash said, "I do love her. Very much. I always have."

Justin looked bewildered. "Then—"

Ash set his hand on the lad's shoulder. "We will continue our discussion later, all right? I have an important meeting to attend. I will return as soon as I can."

Justin's eyes brightened. "Does the meeting have to do with Rosetta?"

"In some ways, aye."

The boy hopped down from the bed and snatched up his weapon. "I am coming with you."

"Nay, Justin."

"I want to help. Most of the knights in the stories have squires. I will serve as your squire for the afternoon." The boy's smile turned cheeky. "I will practice with my bow all day tomorrow, Uncle, if you let me come along."

Ash's brows rose. "*All* day?"

Justin nodded. "I promise. 'Tis not just any old promise, either, but a *solemn* one."

Trying very hard not to chuckle, Ash said, "Very well. Gather what you need for our journey, Squire. I will await you in the bailey."

"What do you mean, Father Stephen is not here?"

The wiry little man behind the open church door shrank back at Edric's brusque tone. "I am sorry, Lord Sherborne. I injured my arm and could not drive the wagon, so he went in my stead. He has gone to buy candles and beeswax polish from the next town."

Edric looked angry enough to kick down the church

wall.

Standing on the portico beside Edric, Rosetta exhaled a sigh of relief. Without the priest to conduct the ceremony, there could be no wedding. Now, she just had to find a way to escape Edric, but he and his men were watching her every single moment.

She still had the dagger that Ash had given her, but she hadn't drawn it. There hadn't been a good opportunity to try and flee. There was no point in attempting to escape unless she had a chance of succeeding. A failed attempt would mean she'd lose the weapon to the men—and Edric might follow through on his threat to kill Ash and Justin.

As Edric swore under his breath, she dug her nails into the back of his hand—he was clutching hers so tightly he might crush her fingers—and forced a smile. "What a shame that we cannot wed today."

He scowled and glanced back at the man inside the church. "You said the priest went to the next town?"

"Aye, milord. He should return by dusk."

"This marriage cannot wait."

"Of course it can," Rosetta said.

"Nay, it cannot, *my love*. We must find the priest and bring him back here."

Rosetta battled a flare of anxiety. "You have no idea what roads he took, Edric. You will never find him."

A calculating smile ticked up the corner of Edric's mouth. "The church roof still needs repairs, does it not?" he asked the man.

"It does, milord. Father Stephen is worried that we will not have it fixed before winter, because we still have not raised all of the funds."

"I will pay for a brand new roof," Edric said, "if you tell us how to get to the places that Father Stephen has gone to visit."

The man's eyes widened. Glancing nervously from

Edric to Rosetta, he said, "'Tis a very generous offer, Lord Sherborne—"

"Good, then 'tis settled."

"Edric," Rosetta snapped. "The wedding is not going to happen."

"My love, I realize you do not want to inconvenience the priest. However, I am sure he will be happy to wed us when he remembers we were denied our marriage days ago due to unexpected circumstances." Edric signaled to two of his guards. "Get the details from this man and go find Father Stephen. Get him here as swiftly as possible, and you will each receive ten pieces of silver."

Rosetta fumed. "Edric, I will *not*—"

"Hush, my love." He released her hand for the barest instant, slid his arm around her waist, and turned her to step down off the portico—so quickly, her head spun. The remaining two men-at-arms followed.

"Edric!" She dug her heels into the dirt, raising a small cloud of dust.

He halted abruptly. As she straightened, he said, "Continue to protest, and I will send my remaining men to Damsley Keep. Is that what you want, Rosetta?"

"You would really murder Ash and Justin?" she asked, refusing to temper her biting tone.

"I really would." For an instant, regret flickered in his eyes. "Their being harmed would not be my fault. 'Twould be entirely yours, for forcing me to take such action."

She gaped, stunned by the twisted logic. "*My* fault?" She tried to find a quelling retort, but he propelled her onward to the wattle-and-daub tavern located close to the church in the town square—a place that rented rooms upstairs to travelers.

Mother Mary, but she had to get away!

The scents of tallow candle smoke and frying fish filled her nostrils as Edric pushed her through the front door. In the shadowed interior, folk seated at tables near the polished wooden bar or the hearth glanced their way, but soon returned to their conversations and drinks.

The tavern owner approached, smiling. "Lord Sherborne. 'Tis a pleasure to see you."

"Is the room ready?" Edric asked.

"Aye, but we were not expecting you so early."

Reaching into the bag tied to his sword belt, Edric took out a few coins and dropped them into the man's palm. "Her ladyship wanted somewhere quiet to rest for a while. I did not think you would mind."

"Not at all." The tavern owner fetched an iron key and handed it to Edric. "Would you care for some wine, milady? Something to eat?"

Rosetta held his kind gaze. If she could secretly ask him for a quill and ink—

"She wants only to rest," Edric answered. He urged her forward, causing her to stumble.

"You are going to break my ankle," Rosetta groused.

Pulling her in closer, he murmured, "Then you cannot run away."

Her stomach clenched at the feel of his breath against her hair. She longed to grab her knife, but the armed men were too close behind. They would overpower her as soon as she drew the dagger. Forcing herself to be patient, she climbed the stairs with Edric to the upper level. He unlocked a door at the far end and pushed her into the room.

Her heart pounding, she glanced about the chamber, dominated by a large bed. Unlit candles were clustered on the bedside tables, the hearth tiles, and on the small trestle table by the door. The floorboards and bed linens were scattered with pink rose petals: the petals of wild, briar roses, just as Ash had promised her for their first romantic night together.

Oh, God. Oh, God.

Bile scalded the back of her mouth, while the door

clicked shut behind her. "I remembered that Ash used to call you his Briar Rose. 'Tis why I chose the rose petals," Edric murmured, walking up behind her. "Do you like the way the room is decorated for us?"

Tears burned her eyes as she put several paces between them, bringing her closer to the shuttered window. "I will not lie with you."

"Our marriage *will* be consummated tonight, Rosetta—whether you are willing or not."

Her trembling hand touched her sleeve, felt the solid weight of Ash's knife beneath the silk. If she was left with no other choice, she would use the dagger to stop Edric from consummating their union.

"I have gone to a lot of trouble for you, my love," Edric said, anger hardening his gaze. "You would be wise to cooperate with me, not fight me."

"I do not love you."

"Rosetta—"

"I will *never* love you the way I love Ash."

Edric laughed bitterly. "So I was right. You do still have feelings for him."

"Stop this madness, and let me go. I will *not* be your wife."

He smiled as if her defiance was pointless. "You do not have any other choice."

Rosetta struggled to remain calm. She would *not* give up on escape. If she was clever, she might be able to use the dagger to break the lock on the door.

"In case you are planning to flee, you cannot leave this chamber. The men-at-arms are standing guard outside the door." Edric gestured to the window. "Try to climb out, and you will be gravely injured or die in the fall to the ground."

Her rage kindled anew. Fighting the blinding urge to lunge at him, she said, "You have obviously thought this through."

Edric shrugged. "I know what I want. That, my love, includes you."

Purely on instinct, she grabbed the nearest candle and hurled it at him. He ducked, ran for the door, and slammed it behind him. His laughter, drifting in from the corridor, mocked her as he turned the key in the lock.

"Ash," Rosetta whispered, tears slipping down her face. "I am sorry." By the time he learned that she hadn't returned to Millenstowe Keep, she'd be married to Edric.

Sobs wrenched up inside her, and she longed to curl up on the bed and weep.

She *mustn't*. The wedding hadn't happened yet. There was still a chance that she could get away.

If she loved Ash—and she did, so very much!—then she mustn't stop fighting for that love until the very last possible moment.

Sucking in slow, steadying breaths, she drew the dagger from her sleeve. The metal glinted in the sunlight streaming in past the closed shutters. As she tucked in the edges of the linen strips tying the knife's sheath to her arm, her gaze shifted to the bed, and then the window.

Hurrying to the shutters, she threw them open and leaned out over the window sill as far as she could. She studied the surrounding exterior wall and the distance to the ground.

Edric was right; 'twas a fair way down to the ground.

That wouldn't stop her, though.

Chapter Fourteen

stride his black destrier, Ash looked down at Justin as they passed the two-story townhomes on the outskirts of Clipston. "Remember, you must stay with me or the men-at-arms at all times."

Justin guided his brown and white pony around a rut in the road; the two armed guards riding in the rear followed the boy's lead. "I know, Uncle. You have told me three times already."

Ash grinned. "I wanted to make very sure you understood."

Justin rolled his eyes.

Turning his attention back to the street ahead, Ash noted how quiet the town was, compared to the last time he'd visited. Without a noble wedding to bring crowds out into the street, folk were either busy indoors or going about their daily chores. A short distance ahead, children shouted, laughed, and tossed wooden blocks into a bucket; Ash spurred his mount ahead of Justin's and then guided it to the side of the street, so as not to disturb their game.

"I am starving," Justin said, his voice carrying over the echoing *clip-clop* of the horses' hooves.

"The men-at-arms can take you to buy a meat pie,"

Ash said over his shoulder. "Then, they will escort you to a spot where you can practice with your bow." While Ash had allowed Justin to come along, he didn't want the boy at his meeting with Rosetta's sire; the information Ash had to share was far too dangerous.

"Can I get the pie soon?"

"Aye. In a few moments, when we reach the town square, we will go separate ways. The baker's shop is in the square."

"Good. I did not realize that being your squire would make me so hungry."

Ash chuckled. Justin had done an admirable job as squire so far. Mayhap the boy was more ready to begin his training as a page than Ash had thought.

The road opened into the town square, the old stone church directly ahead. In his missive, Ash had advised Lord Montgomery to meet him under the towering oak at the far corner of the church cemetery. They would ride on together from there to the meadow by the river, a suitably remote spot to have their discussion, and, if his lordship desired, Ash would take him to the site where Rosetta had found her ring. Ash had already forewarned his guards that they would be responsible for Justin for a while.

Ash headed for the side of the church, where he would have a clear view of the oak. Lord Montgomery was there, waiting. Ash raised his hand in greeting. His lordship answered in kind.

Halting his destrier, Ash turned it to face his men and Justin. "We will meet up outside the baker's shop later this afternoon."

"Aye, milord," the guards said.

Justin, however, wasn't paying any heed. He was staring at the tavern.

"Justin," Ash said.

The boy didn't immediately face forward. "Uncle—"

"Squire," Ash said, more sternly. "You are supposed to listen."

Frowning, Justin pointed to a window on the building's upper level. "Why is Rosetta in the tavern?"

Rosetta turned away from the window, hurried to the bed, and yanked aside the blankets, sending wilting petals flying to the floor. A shame to ruin perfectly good sheets, but she would ensure the tavern owner was paid for his loss.

With the dagger, she cut wide strips of cloth from the top sheet. Her hands shaking, she braided the fabric, working as quickly as she could. There was no telling when Edric would return. When he unlocked the door, she wanted to be long gone.

Raised voices carried from down in the town square. Was Edric railing at the poor man at the church again, or had he found someone else to scorn?

She tied the lengths of braided linen together, realizing as she did so that she hadn't made the makeshift rope long enough. Cursing under her breath, she cut more cloth.

Hurry. Hurry!

Again, cries rose from outside. The rumble of a passing cart distorted the sound, but still, one of the voices sounded like Ash's.

Hope bloomed inside her, urging her to run to the window. She crushed the foolish emotion. Ash wouldn't be in the town; he was at Damsley Keep. Her frantic mind was playing tricks on her.

Exhaling an unsteady breath, she grabbed her linen rope.

A dull *thud* came from outside the window. Was someone throwing stones?

She moved to the window, just as an object sailed through. She squeaked and stumbled back, as an arrow landed on the floorboards.

She recognized the arrow. 'Twas one of Justin's.

Ash stared up at the woman leaning out over the sill. Justin was right; 'twas most certainly Rosetta, still garbed in the cloak and gown she'd worn when she'd ridden away with Edric.

What in hellfire was she doing in Clipston?

"Uncle, why is—?"

"I do not know, but I will find out."

Rosetta disappeared back inside the tavern. Misgiving roiled inside Ash as he spurred his horse closer to the building, for his gut instinct, which had never failed him, told him she was in trouble. "Rosetta!" he called.

"Rosetta!" Justin shouted, his voice blending with Ash's.

She didn't reappear. Mayhap she hadn't heard them?

"Rosetta!" Ash cried again.

Still, she didn't come to the window. Someone— likely Edric—could be preventing her from answering, or she could have left the chamber. Fury welled up inside Ash in a violent tempest. Even if it turned out that his instinct was wrong, that all was well, he wanted to know why she was in the tavern and not on her way to Millenstowe Keep as arranged.

Justin swung down from his pony. "Since I am your squire, I will go inside and—"

161

"Wait." Ash dismounted to stand with the boy. "'Tis a gallant offer, but we cannot just barge into the tavern. We do not know who else is inside, and we might put Rosetta in danger."

The boy's eyes lit with understanding. "Chivalrous knights must always put the lady's safety first."

"Exactly."

Remembering that Lord Montgomery was waiting for him, Ash turned to his men. "Go to the church cemetery and fetch his lordship. Tell him to bring his guards."

As his men-at-arms rode off, Ash studied the window again. If he could somehow climb up the outside wall and peer in, to see what was going on inside—

"I have an idea, Uncle."

"Mmm?" Ash scratched his chin while his mind calculated the best way to scale the wall.

"I can fire an arrow through the window. She will know we are here."

God's bones!

"If anyone besides Rosetta is in the room, they will likely come to the window. I will act as though I am just a witless six-year-old who has no idea how to use a bow, and that I fired the arrow into the building by accident."

"'Tis a brilliant idea. Do it," Ash said.

Justin nocked an arrow, aimed, and fired. The arrow hit the wall near the window and dropped to the ground.

Damnation! Ash bit the inside of his cheek and fought the urge to take the bow and fire it himself.

Justin growled with frustration and nocked another arrow.

"Lower your right arm," Ash said as the boy aimed. "A little more… Fire!"

The arrow sailed through the open window.

Rosetta picked up the arrow and ran to the sill. Ash stood below, Justin beside him.

Oh, thank God!

She smiled, fighting tears. "I am so glad to see you."

"What are you doing in Clipston?" Ash called up to her.

"Edric is going to force me to marry him. Today."

Ash's face darkened with rage. "The conniving—" His hand dropped to the hilt of his sword.

"There are two armed guards at my door," she cut in. "The only way for me to leave is by the window." She held up her braided cloth rope. "I made this, but I have nowhere to secure it—"

"Is there a heavy table in your chamber? Or a bed?" Ash asked.

The bed. Of course.

She left the window and tied one end of her rope to the bed frame. Returning to the sill, she tossed the other end out. It tumbled down to hang several yards above the ground.

As she grabbed her voluminous skirts, readying to climb out, she heard a key grating in the lock. Edric was returning.

With a frantic gasp, she put both hands on the sill and swung one leg over. The silk of her gown snagged on rough wood.

The chamber door opened. "Rosetta!" Edric cried.

He ran to her, his footfalls as loud as the hammering of her heart. She caught hold of the rope and tried to get her other leg over, but her skirts were firmly caught. Snarling, he seized her arm and hauled her back into the room. Fabric tore.

She screeched as she fell hard on the floorboards.

"Edric!" Ash bellowed from the ground below.

An arrow plowed into the edge of the window.

Reaching back, Edric yanked up the rope, tossed it on the planks, and slammed the shutters. As she scrambled to get to her feet, her shoes sliding on yards of slippery fabric, he hauled her up. "What were you trying to do? Kill yourself?"

"I was trying to get away from *you*!" Rosetta lunged sideways, grabbing for the dagger still lying on the ruined sheet, but he got to it first and tossed it under the bed, out of her reach.

"If you are wise, you will let me go," Rosetta said very firmly. "Ash is here—"

"He will not stop our marriage. I just received word that my men found the priest. They are on their way here." Edric grabbed her arm as shouts reached her from the tavern's lower level: Ash was coming for her.

Rosetta fought Edric's hold, twisting her arm to try and break free. When he refused to let go and attempted to draw his sword, she walloped him hard across the face. He grimaced, but his brutal grip didn't ease at all.

Pounding footfalls sounded on the tavern staircase, followed by the *clang* of clashing weapons. Judging by the noise, men were battling on the other side of the door.

"Ash!" she shrieked.

Sweat coated Edric's brow. Drawing his sword, he said, "Now, you are going to walk—"

The chamber door smashed inward. Ash stood on the threshold, his sword gleaming. He glared at Edric.

"Release her," he growled, "or die."

Chapter Fifteen

Ash shook with the force of his fury. Edric was holding Rosetta's arm so tightly, she'd have nasty bruises. She was obviously terrified, and seeing her so afraid made his rage boil to the point of near overflowing.

Tightening his grip on his sword, Ash fought the agonizing pain in his right hand. Naught—especially not his own discomfort—would stand in the way of him rescuing Rosetta. "I told you to release her, Edric."

The bastard scowled. "*You* will stand aside."

"Like hell I will. Rosetta is *mine*."

"Not anymore."

Ash stared Edric down. "I will not ask again. Let her go."

Edric's defiant gaze slid past Ash to the corridor, where his unconscious soldiers were being dragged away by Ash's men-at-arms. If Edric had hoped for help from his lackeys, he'd not get it.

Ash had also asked Lord Montgomery and Justin to clear all of the folk from the lower level, to save them from being caught up in the fight; it also prevented Edric from bribing them for help. The sound of Lord Montgomery's commanding voice along with the scraping of chairs and the banging of the main door confirmed the tavern was being emptied.

Seizing the advantage of her captor's distraction, Rosetta bolted sideways. She wrenched free of Edric's grip, and he grabbed again for her, but she darted back toward the window, her only means of escape.

Ash lunged. Edric raised his sword, and the weapons clashed, just as sunlight flooded into the chamber. Rosetta had opened the shutters.

"Go down the rope," Ash shouted to her. "*Go!*"

"A-all right."

Edric swore and stepped backward toward the window.

Ash curled his free hand into a fist. He *had* to keep Edric away from Rosetta.

"You should have known your plan would fail," Ash goaded, drawing Edric's focus once again. The pain in Ash's right hand was nigh unbearable, but he would not yield in his duty to protect Rosetta.

"'Tis not over yet." Edric took another backward step, his foot sliding on crushed petals.

Rushing forward, Ash brought his sword down in a glinting arc. He gasped as Edric deflected the strike and retaliated with several driving blows that forced Ash back toward the door.

"I will stop you from marrying her," Ash vowed.

"Not if you are dead."

Ash laughed, the sound full of mockery. "You do not have the mettle to kill me. Otherwise you would have slain me on Crusade."

Wariness flickered across Edric's features.

"Instead, you just cut me. A half-finished job."

Edric glanced at the window, as did Ash. Rosetta was poised to climb down.

"Please, my love," Edric said, longing in his voice, "I care about you—"

She threw her betrothal ring onto the floor. "You care only for yourself." She pulled her skirts over the sill and vanished from view.

A violent cry broke from Edric. Eyes blazing, his face flushed with anger, he rounded on Ash, his sword lashing again and again. Steel clashed and clanged. Step by step, Ash lured him out of the chamber. As Ash cleared the threshold, Edric rushed at him.

Ash spun, his back hitting the upstairs banister. He neatly avoided the strike, while Edric tripped on a sword that must have belonged to one of his men. Edric lost his balance, but swiftly straightened to deflect a ringing blow from Ash.

"Rosetta was right," Ash said, breathing hard. "You are a selfish bastard."

"Why is that? Because I love her?"

Ash attacked again. He lunged, parried, kept up his relentless assault until his men-at-arms had hauled Edric's soldiers outside and the front door had swung shut behind them. "Be honest, Edric. You want the gold."

"Gold?" Edric wiped sweat from his face. "What gold?"

"You know bloody well what gold." Ash thrust hard with his sword, forcing Edric to the top of the stairwell. "Admit it, 'twas your plan all along. Marry Rosetta, wait for her sire to die so you could claim his lands where the riches are likely buried. Or, mayhap, even hurry things along by killing Lord Montgomery yourself?"

An indignant cry sounded from below. Daring a glance, Ash saw his lordship standing near the bottom of the stairs. Justin, however, was nowhere in sight. Neither was Rosetta. He hoped she'd made it safely down the rope to the ground. If she had fallen and been hurt...

As Edric attacked again, Ash drew upon his seething fury to deliver a swift, punishing blow. Edric slipped, and he tumbled backward down several stairs, unable to stop his fall. His sword fell from his hand and slid down several more stairs, out of his reach. Sprawled against the banister, he struggled to rise.

Ash was on him in an instant, his sword pointed at Edric's throat.

His breaths hissing between his teeth, Edric glared up at Ash.

"Admit to the truth," Ash demanded.

"I have told you the truth," Edric said.

"You have not. Confess," Ash roared, the sword pressing against Edric's skin. If he didn't coerce the truth from the whoreson now, he might never have the chance again.

The creak of a lower stair marked Lord Montgomery's approach. "Since I seem to be involved in this matter you are discussing, can I ask what the hell is going on?"

"Milord, you must help me. Ash's jealousy has driven him mad," Edric said, his eyes wild. "He insists he is entitled to marry Rosetta."

Lord Montgomery frowned. "Ash?"

"Do not heed him, milord," Ash said, maintaining the threat of his sword. "Edric is a lying, treacherous, manipulative—"

"Ash!" Shock whitened his lordship's features. "To speak of a peer, a champion of the Crusades, in such a foul way—"

"Thank you, milord, for believing me." Edric grimaced. "Help me, please, before—"

A draft gusted up the stairs as the tavern door opened. Rosetta strode in, carrying a rolled parchment. Justin walked beside her, holding his bow. Seeing them safe sent a flood of relief rippling through Ash.

Rosetta reached her father's side. Justin halted at the bottom of the stairs.

"My love," Edric called. "I was worried about you—"

"Were you? Well, you will be glad to know that I am fine, apart from a torn gown." Her gaze shifted to Ash, while she discreetly lifted the parchment and tipped her head toward Justin.

Ah. What she'd found should not be discussed in front of the boy.

Keeping his gaze trained on Edric, Ash said, "Justin, I have a very important task for you; one I cannot entrust to anyone else."

"Aye, Uncle?"

"I want you to find the town sheriff and bring him here. Take one of the men-at-arms with you. Agreed, Squire?"

"Agreed."

"Good. Go now." The boy hurried from the tavern.

As soon as Justin had gone, Rosetta unfurled the parchment. The thin, cured skin bore a copy of Ash's sketch of the ring Rosetta had found.

"God's bones," Ash muttered.

"'Twas in Edric's saddlebag," she said. "There were other parchments, too."

Edric's face paled, and he looked about to be ill.

"Where did you get the drawing?" Ash demanded.

"Where do you think?" Edric groused.

"You found it in my chamber at Millenstowe Keep."

"Millenstowe?" Lord Montgomery asked, obviously puzzled.

"This happened years ago, when we were squires at your castle, milord," Ash said. He nudged Edric's leg with his boot. "Well?"

"All right!" Edric snapped. "That day, I knew you and Rosetta had found something that you did not want to share with me. I...resented being left out. When you went to your chamber, I waited outside. You spent a while in there and then, when you left, I stole inside. I saw ink stains on your table and guessed you had written on parchment. When I found the drawing, I made a copy for myself."

Lord Montgomery was studying the drawing. "'Tis a ring."

"One made of gold, with a red stone and strange designs etched into the band. I still have it," Rosetta said. "'Tis in a safe place."

"You had heard the local tales of a vast hoard to be found in these lands, Edric," Ash pressed. "You knew the treasure was likely buried on his lordship's estate."

"I guessed, aye," Edric muttered.

"You wanted those riches enough to kill for them."

"Now you are accusing me of murder?"

"Aye. When you learned of the peasant who had dug up the ancient coin with his vegetables, you paid thugs to beat him for information and then kill him. To your great disappointment, though, you did not get hold of the coin; I was lucky to end up with it."

"You!" Edric choked out.

"There was also the gold belt buckle. You paid men to kill the poor man who found it, did you not? You wanted to silence all news of the findings, so that no one else could figure out where the treasure was buried and unearth it before you did."

Edric was silent a moment, and then he chortled, as if greatly amused. "What a fantastical tale you have woven, Ash."

"'Tis not a tale," Rosetta said coolly. "The copy of the drawing proves you had an interest in the gold."

"He also had an interest in you, Rosetta," Ash added.

"One that was far from romantic."

Anger glinted in Edric's eyes again.

"He needed to marry you, Briar Rose, because then he could take ownership of the land where the riches are likely hidden."

"My father would have to die first, though, for him to lay claim," Rosetta said with a frown.

"I vow he had considered that obstacle," Ash said. "How would his lordship have died, Edric? Poison in his wine? An unfortunate accident while out riding his horse? Or mayhap he would be attacked by thieves lurking in the woods?"

Lord Montgomery scowled. "Did you plan such wickedness? Well, did you?"

Edric sneered. "What I planned was to have the life I damned well deserved. A beautiful wife, riches to buy whatever I desired—"

"—and John Lackland as England's new King?" Ash added.

Edric's mouth snapped shut.

"I know you are a traitor," Ash said. "I know you are working to overthrow King Richard, and that the treasure was to be used to pay for a rebellion."

His gaze frosty, Edric said, "You have proof of my treachery?"

"I do."

A strangled cry broke past Edric's lips. "Damn you, Ash. Damn you to hell, for you have ruined all!"

"I have, and gladly so." Ash indulged in a bitter smile. "You intended to eliminate me long ago, did you not? On Crusade, when I said I intended to return home and marry Rosetta, you saw the threat to your plan to claim the buried riches. You waited for the right moment, and then you attacked me."

"Attacked you?" Lord Montgomery's voice

171

roughened with horror. "*He* is responsible for that scar on your brow?"

Edric averted his gaze.

"He is, milord. He also injured my hands."

"God above!" his lordship muttered.

"You cut me with the Saracen weapon, Edric," Ash continued, the words pouring out of him as if they'd been dammed up for far too long, "but at the last moment, you could not slay me. I saw that flicker of indecision in your eyes, before you turned and ran. You expected me to die from my wounds; that they would become corrupted and I would never survive the fever. Since you returned to England before I did, no doubt you thought I had died in the East, until you learned that I had been granted Damsley Keep." Ash tsked. "What a shock that must have been for you. Around that time, your father also died, did he not, making you lord of Wallensford Keep? Was that not when you insisted on finalizing your plans to marry Rosetta?"

"There were rumors about Lord Sherborne's death." Lord Montgomery said. "He appeared to have died in his sleep, but some said that he had been murdered. Smothered by a feather pillow, I believe."

"I heard similar rumors," Ash said. Holding Edric's gaze, he asked, "Was he murdered?"

Edric shrugged.

"Answer the question," Lord Montgomery growled. "Did you murder your sire?"

His expression mutinous, Edric remained silent.

"Speak!" his lordship commanded, his voice booming in the tavern. "You are a knight, are you not? A man who swore an oath to uphold the principles of chivalry? If you have even the slightest shred of honor remaining in you—"

"Fine. I did it," Edric shouted. "I killed my father. I wanted the gold. I attacked Ash."

Relief washed through Ash. *Finally*, an admission of guilt.

"I regret that I ever granted you permission to wed my daughter," Lord Montgomery said. "You will never marry Rosetta. *Never.*"

She moved closer, part of her gown dragging on the stairs. "Tell me, Edric. Why did you cut Ash's face and hands?"

Edric stared up at her, his expression one of a man who had lost all that had driven him to succeed. "You really do not know?"

"I want to hear it from you," she answered, her tone softened by anguish.

"Ash gazed into your lovely eyes, so I cut his face. He touched your skin and your hair, so I slashed his hands. He held you in his arms and kissed you—"

"You hurt him because he *loved* me?"

"I hurt him because you were to be mine."

Ash sensed Rosetta's pained gaze upon him, but he didn't dare take his focus from Edric.

The tavern door opened. "Uncle, I brought the sheriff," Justin called.

"Good," Ash called back. "Sheriff, if you will—"

Edric kicked Ash hard in the leg, causing him to waver. The sword nicked Edric's throat, but he ignored the bleeding cut and threw himself sideways down the stairs. He grabbed for his sword.

Ash lunged for Edric, but Lord Montgomery was faster. He snatched up the weapon and with the flat of the blade, whacked Edric across the back of the head. With a groan, Edric collapsed, unconscious.

"Ash!" Rosetta ran up the stairs between them and threw her arms around him.

He kissed her cheek, her hair, and hugged her tight. Ah, God, how glad he was that she was finally safe. He longed to kiss her, to show her how much he loved her, but he was well aware that such affection might not be appropriate in front of her father.

"Will someone please tell me what is going on?" the sheriff said.

"I will be glad to," Lord Montgomery replied from where he stood guard over Edric.

As the sheriff and Rosetta's sire started talking, Ash eased her to arm's length. Her eyes were shining with love. There was so much he wanted to say to her—

He felt a tug on his sleeve.

"Uncle?" Justin said, standing beside him.

"Aye?"

"What we did today was even more exciting than those old stories. I am glad we were able to rescue Rosetta."

"So am I," Ash said.

"And so am I." Smiling, Rosetta drew the boy in close for a group hug. "I owe you both my thanks. You are the finest, bravest heroes this damsel has ever known."

Chapter Sixteen

Rosetta paused with Ash and her father near the circle of ancient standing stones. Afternoon sun cast gold over the monument and the surrounding field. The wheat had been harvested days ago; sheaves dried in the sun.

A short distance away, the creek glinted, inviting her to stay and swim as she, Ash, and Edric had done long ago. So much had changed for all three of them since those days. While she despised Edric for all that he had done and had conspired to do, it had been difficult to see him chained and hauled away. He would be imprisoned in the town gaol before being taken to London for trial in the King's Courts.

She'd promised to give the sheriff a full written account of all she knew about Edric's deceptions, as had Ash and her sire. On her father's insistence, though, they had agreed not to include any mention of the gold. He'd vowed that 'twas too dangerous, especially when they had no idea who would end up reading the accounts and whether those officials were trustworthy or not; 'twas safest to keep the treasure a secret. That still left her with plenty to write about. Edric must be held accountable for his selfishness and cruelty.

Brushing past her, Justin pointed to the creek. "Can I go down to the water, Uncle?"

"You may. See if you can find any fish."

The boy ran across the field, his feet churning up loose dirt. She laughed, for she knew just how good it felt to be young and to race down to the water.

Ash entwined his fingers with hers; from the warmth in his eyes, he remembered, too.

"Show me where you found the ring," her father said.

Together, she and Ash walked along the well-trodden foot path that had had been there as long as she remembered. She stopped partway and looked about. "'Twas somewhere around here."

Her sire halted and gazed up at the standing stones. "The jewel must have been near the surface. 'Twas likely washed here by heavy rains."

Beside her, Ash went very still. "You mean—?"

Lord Montgomery's mouth curved in a knowing smile. "I have known about the riches for years, and have done my utmost to protect them."

"You *know* where the treasure is buried?" Rosetta asked. How silly she now felt for keeping her finding of the ring a secret from him.

Her sire nodded. "'Tis under the fallen stone in the middle of the circle."

"God's blood!" Ash whispered. "To think how many times we have visited the stones, Rosetta, and had no idea what was beneath our feet."

"How did you find it, Father?"

"Oh, I did not find it myself. Years ago, I hired a stonemason to repair Millenstowe Keep's outer wall. I did not realize—and I would never have approved of it if I had known—but he and his three apprentices decided to use one of the standing stones. They managed to topple it over, but when they peered into the hole in the ground left by the stone, they saw gold. I happened to be inspecting fields that day, and the head mason ran to me, almost too excited to speak. When I saw the riches…" Lord Montgomery sighed. "I knew what a perilous situation had arisen. If word of the gold got out, my fields would be crowded with folk trying to find the hoard. My crops would be ruined, and there would be an increase in fights, thefts, and murders on my lands. More importantly, the gold could be used to manipulate the balance of power in England."

"As it still can," Ash added gravely.

"Aye. I remembered how things were when I wed your mother, Rosetta. William the Conqueror had taken control of England more than a hundred years earlier, but animosity between folk of Norman and Saxon bloodlines persisted. Some of the older folk longed for an armed rebellion to oust the Normans and return England to the way it had been under Saxon rule."

"Surely the Normans had governed England for too long for there to be any chance of ousting them?" Rosetta asked.

"One would believe so, and yet, the old hatred was very real. The marriage between your mother, a Norman, and I, a Saxon, was arranged to help eradicate the animosity that lingered. While she and I resented the marriage at first, we soon fell in love, in part because we both believed in the importance of peace. I still believe 'tis the best thing for England—which is why I want the riches to remain in the ground. Of course, every now and again, a bit of gold is discovered, which renews interest in finding the hoard, but luckily, most folk are convinced by now that the rumors of great riches are no more than tales."

"I understand, Father, but how did you keep the stonemasons from talking about their find? Surely they would have told their friends."

"I paid them very well to fill in the hole where they

had found the riches and to move the stone to cover it. A few pieces of gold likely did not get buried very deep, such as your ring. I also ordered them to leave Warwickshire, and threatened to have them arrested if they were seen in this area again."

"So far, your plan has been successful," Ash noted.

"I pray it remains so. I do have more men patrolling this area than other parts of my estate, and they have orders to ward off anyone who is too curious about the stone circle. I also inspect the monument every month or so, to ensure all remains in order."

"I will never reveal where the gold is hidden," Rosetta said.

"Nor will I," Ash said.

"Good." Lord Montgomery glanced down the field to where Justin stood knee-deep in the water. "I suppose I should go and keep him from getting thoroughly muddy and soaked."

Laughing, Ash said, "You can *try*."

"We will see how I have done when I return with him." Lord Montgomery's smile turned knowing once again, and his eyes sparkled. "By then, you two also might have some news for me."

"News?" Rosetta asked.

Her father winked and strode away down the path.

She frowned at Ash. "Am I the only one who has no idea what he meant?"

Ash chuckled. "Do not be upset. You will know soon enough."

As Ash tugged on Rosetta's hand, excitement and

dread warred within him. What he had to show her, to say to her, was important, and he didn't want to muddle his words.

Ah, God, but if she recoiled in horror…

He forced his disquiet aside as hand in hand, they walked to the stone circle. He gestured for her to sit on the flat stone, and when she did, he sat down beside her. The breeze whispered through the stones, stirring her hair and lending her cheeks a rosy flush.

She fingered windblown hair from her cheek, while he leaned forward, his arms resting on his knees. He clenched and unclenched his gloved hands, easing some of the pain that remained from the swordfight earlier. How did he begin? He couldn't just blurt out what he wanted to say; he was a chivalrous knight, after all.

"This place is very special to me," Ash finally said, tracing a seam on his glove with his thumb.

"To me as well."

"I knew it had to be the place where…" He looked down at the ground by his boots.

"Where the treasure was buried?"

"Nay, where I…" He took a steadying breath and then caught hold of the fingers of his left glove. And pulled.

As sunlight touched his bare hand, revealing the lines of scarring, misshapen flesh, and buckled skin, a hard knot of revulsion filled his throat. His other hand was just as awful. He was hideous. Monstrous. Whatever had made him think she would want to see him the way he was now?

She made a small sound—one of distress, no doubt. He should spare her any more horror. His hands shaking, he struggled to put his glove back on, but her hand closed over his, stopping him.

Her skin was smooth against his damaged flesh. *Smooth. Soft. Warm.* A despairing laugh welled within him. How long had it been since he'd felt anything with his hand apart from the inside of his glove?

He dared to glance at her, and tears glistened in her eyes.

"I apologize," he muttered. "I thought 'twas best… I wanted…"

"I am glad you showed me," she whispered.

"You were right. 'Tis who I am now." The urge to yank his glove back on, to hide his disfigurement, rose within him to near panic. "I wanted you to know…to see…"

She curled her fingers through his, drawing a groan from him. Then she brought his hand to her lips and kissed it.

He gasped, stunned, as she gently, lovingly kissed his scars, his fingers, and his palm. Then, setting his hand on her skirt, she carefully removed his other glove. How liberating it felt to feel the leather slip away and the fresh breeze cool his skin. How wondrous her touch felt. "You are not appalled by my hands?" he rasped.

"Why should I be?" she said with a tearful smile. "You are even more of a hero to me now than you were years ago."

"I am scarred."

"So am I, in my own ways. Neither of us is the same person we were years ago."

"But—"

"I am very proud of the man you have become, Ash." Tears trailed down her cheeks as she whispered, "I love you. I always will."

He dropped to his knees on the dirt and took her hand in both of his. He *had* to ask her; he couldn't wait a moment longer. "Rosetta, will you do me the honor of marrying me?"

She quivered in his grasp. How he hoped she wasn't readying to turn him down.

"I promise I will be a good husband to you. At the tavern, while you were speaking with the sheriff, I asked your father for your hand in marriage. He granted me permission to wed you."

She sniffled. "Oh, Ash—"

"I love you, Rosetta. Please say you will be my wife. *Please.*"

She leaned forward and kissed him on the lips. "I will."

Joy surged through him. He kissed her back, his tongue delving into the warmth of her mouth. Their kisses deepened, slowed, reaffirmed their long ago promises to one another that they would be together forever.

At last, Rosetta sighed against his mouth. Drawing back slightly, she mock frowned at him. "You realize I have just agreed to be both a wife *and* a mother."

"True." Ash's brows rose. "Are you changing your mind?"

"Not at all. I adore Justin."

Grinning, Ash said, "He is going to be thrilled."

Her smile softened. "Not as thrilled as I am, by far." She wrapped her arms around his neck and kissed him again, and with a lusty growl, Ash sank his right hand into her tresses. *Coolness. Silken softness.* True love.

God's blood, but he was a lucky man.

Epilogue

The town of Clipston
Warwickshire, England
Late August, 1192

Adjusting her grip on the reins of her white mare, Rosetta raised her veiled head, smiled, and waved to the cheering crowds on either side of the town street. The musicians, walking ahead of her and her six armed guards, played a merry melody on flutes, pipes, and a tabor as they led her toward the stone church in the town square.

There, Ash would be waiting for her.

There, they would be joined in holy matrimony, with Justin, Herta, her parents, and dear friends as witnesses. Afterward, the guests would be carted to Damsley Keep for a sumptuous feast, dancing, and boisterous celebration that would carry on long into the night.

Excitement tingled through Rosetta as she smoothed the folds of her mother's sumptuous blue cloak. The shimmering pale gold of her new wedding gown, specially made by a local tailor, peeked from underneath. She'd chosen gold because the color reminded her of the buried treasure, of love, and of sunlight, including the afternoon sunshine in which she'd first seen Ash's damaged hands—and that had warmed her and Ash as they'd professed their undying love for one another.

How she loved him, with every bit of her heart and soul.

"Milady! Milady." Peasant children ran alongside her mare and offered her bouquets of wildflowers. Murmuring her thanks, she took them and tucked them under the front of her saddle, beside the ribbon-wrapped bouquet of wild roses that she'd found in her chamber at Millenstowe Keep, where she had lived while counting down the days until she married Ash. She knew without doubt that he had sent the flowers to her, and she hadn't wanted to leave them behind, especially when they matched the crown of wild rose blooms holding her veil in place.

She continued to smile and wave as the procession continued through the streets, until at last, the church came into view. As she rode toward the portico, a shiver ran through her, for she felt so many expectant gazes upon her.

Ash, resplendent in an embroidered dark blue tunic, hose, and black knee-high boots, stood on the portico beside the priest who was holding a leather-bound book. Justin was a few steps away. The boy's hair was remarkably tidy, and his garments were clean and new. Her heart warmed, for she could imagine the effort it had taken Ash to get the boy to look so groomed.

As she and Ash locked gazes across the short distance that separated them, delicious heat trailed through her, for tonight, she would lie with him and finally be his, as she'd always dreamed.

He grinned in that roguish, lop-sided way that made her stomach somersault, and she smiled back.

Rosetta's parents were near the portico, too. Her mother, wearing an exquisite green gown, smiled and wiped her eyes with a handkerchief; she might be of fierce Norman heritage, but she cried at every wedding. Rosetta's father stepped forward to take the mare's reins and help her dismount.

She took the rose bouquet from her saddle and walked to the portico.

Ash winked at her. "Good day, Wife."

"Good day, Husband."

"What lovely flowers."

"They are. My husband is a very thoughtful man."

He smiled and slipped his fingers into hers. He hadn't worn gloves since he'd taken them off at the stone circle, and she was glad.

As they took their places before the priest, her garments rustled, the sound akin to the wind whispering past the towering stones of the ancient monument. Her love for Ash had come full circle. She reveled in the joy that filled her heart, for no hidden riches could ever bring such happiness.

Indeed, the greatest treasure in her life was, and always would be, Ash.

Turn the page for an excerpt from *An Outlaw's Desire*, Book 2 of the *Lost Riches* series.

An Outlaw's Desire

Lost Riches Series Book 2

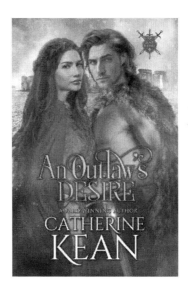

Days before Christmas, Pitt Rutherford is blackmailed into planning an attack on Millenstowe Keep. He discovers, however, that Lady Blythe Welborne, the only woman he's ever truly loved, is within the castle's walls.

As the attack draws ever near, Pitt must choose whether his obligation to claim a legendary treasure is worth more than a second chance at true love.

Print ISBN: 9798712687381
eBook ASIN: B08WHBND1R

Prologue

Millenstowe Keep
Warwickshire, England
Early December, 1185

"Why did the guards leave us on our own?" Fifteen-year-old Lady Blythe Welborne folded her arms over the front of her green wool cloak. A deeper chill settled in the shadows of the towering standing stones surrounding her, for the armed men on duty had walked out of view.

They'd left her with Pitt Rutherford.

Unchaperoned.

Her heart drummed with uncertainty and excitement as wild as the winter wind whispering through the ancient site. At long last, were she and the squire alone?

With swaggered strides, Pitt closed the few steps between them. His straight, dark-brown hair, always untidy, lent a roguishness to his features. "Worry not. All will be well."

His smile and words were doubtless meant to reassure. For years, though, her parents and tutors had impressed upon her the importance of following the rules of propriety. Ignoring the rules could ruin a lady's reputation and her chances of a good marriage.

Blythe respected such rules were set for a reason. Her best friend Rosetta's father, Lord Milton Montgomery, had greatly honored Blythe's family by taking her in as his ward at Millenstowe Keep. As her mother had said, many young ladies wished to complete their tutelage in his lordship's household, and Blythe should be grateful she'd been chosen.

At this moment, though, Blythe cared not about the honor. Finally—oh, finally!—she and Pitt were alone.

A flush tingled over Blythe's skin as he halted a hand's span away from her. Anticipation became a sweet, hot ache.

She'd met the squire, also fifteen years of age, weeks ago in the bailey. She and Rosetta had been walking to the gardens when Blythe's cloak pin had come loose and fallen in the mud. Dashing away from the other squires gathered near the well, he'd retrieved her pin, wiped it clean, and they'd exchanged pleasantries. They'd become friends, and soon after, she'd dreamed of being in his arms, for his keen brown eyes seemed to see the forbidden longings in her soul.

With her leather-gloved hand, she pushed windblown hair from her cheek and gazed up at him, staring down at her. His hungry gaze sent a thrill racing through her. Now that she and Pitt were alone, did she dare to indulge her longings? Oh, how she wanted to. Rosetta had kissed Ash, her handsome squire, at the stone circle. Rosetta had told of the pleasure of that kiss, and now Blythe had the chance at such bliss, too.

His mouth ticking up at one corner, Pitt pulled off his gloves and stroked his fingers down her cheek; the gentlest of caresses. But, the glide of his warm fingertips on her cool skin set aflame every part of her body. Her eyelids fluttered, and she drew a sharp breath.

How did his touch hold such power? If he touched her like that again, she'd never be able to resist—regardless of the consequences. But, she didn't want either of them to get into trouble.

"Pitt," she said. "How can you be sure all will be well?"

"I am friends with one of the guards. I told him about us."

Her breathing turned shallow; eager. She longed to throw herself into Pitt's arms and kiss him. *Really* kiss him, without a single care to hold her back, and with all of the desire and joy gathered within her. Heat swirled up inside her to remember how they'd kissed in the stairwell the other day; frantic kisses with her hands clawing in his hair, his fingers running over her waist and hips. However, they'd promised to keep their relationship secret.

They had to.

Soon, she'd be wed to a well-respected lord almost forty years her senior. She'd had no say in the marriage, didn't want to marry the man, but couldn't defy a union arranged by the crown. Such disobedience would cast dishonor upon her family as well as Lord Montgomery. She'd not disappoint her parents or his lordship.

Dismay settled inside her; she must refuse her squire. Uncrossing her arms, Blythe glanced at where she'd last seen the guards. "Pitt—"

"I promise, we will do no more than kiss." He leaned in and pressed his lips to her brow.

She shivered. Such a tender brush of his mouth, but her body had gone deliciously tingly all over.

Her half-lidded gaze slid to his mouth, the evenness of his teeth, and her belly swooped to remember his lips crushing down on hers in the stairwell, his breath warming her cheek, his body pinning her against the stone wall.

Whatever he'd stirred up within her that day still smoldered within her like a kind of fire: hot, bright, and enticing. She wanted him to kiss her like that again. Over and over and over.

"My friend understands." Pitt caressed her cheek again. "He remembers being young and in love."

Do not let this chance slip away. Take it!

"When he and his colleague are returning, he will forewarn us by raising his voice."

Yearning sharpened to urgent need. Soon, she'd be forever bound to an older lord. Why not take what *she* wanted now?

Again, the breeze blew strands of her hair into her eyes. Before she could brush them away, Pitt's fingers were there, sweeping them aside and tucking them, so gently, behind her ear. His puzzled gaze searched hers.

"I thought you'd be pleased."

"Oh, I am."

"If you do not want to be alone with me—"

"I do. I—"

Take the chance!

She leaned up and pressed her mouth to his.

He groaned, a sound of pleasure. His arms locked around her waist and pulled her flush against him. Her hands curled into the front of his cloak as she gave into the maelstrom of desire inside her.

The looming stones around them faded in focus. All she knew, tasted, sensed, was Pitt.

This is what she wanted every day for the rest of her life. His kiss, his embrace, held the power to meld all the tangled feelings inside her into one goal: to be his.

The fire within her burned hotter.

Pitt sighed against her lips. His kisses deepened, and he nudged even closer, coaxing her to move backward, until her back pressed against the standing stone behind her. As she melted against the monolith, his fingers sank into her hair. He held her head still, while he kept her against the cool stone with his kisses and his body.

Kissing him back with all the passion in her soul, she vowed to remember forever this glorious moment. No one—not even her wedded husband—could ever wrest it from her.

She tasted sweet, perfect, and of every dream he'd ever imagined.

Pitt shuddered as the hunger within him burned hotter. Deepening the kiss, he caught her quick intake of breath, felt her quiver against him, and he sighed again, the sound blending into a growl.

She stilled, clearly unsure. Of course, being a well-bred lady, she had no knowledge of carnal passion. She was still a virgin, while he was not. He paused, his mouth hovering over hers, and their breaths mingled. Blood pounded in his veins. His fingers curled against the curve of her waist; he remembered the silkiness of her gown when he'd touched her in the stairwell, and how the fabric had held the heat of her body. With a silent oath, he drew his arm away and pressed his palm to the weathered stone behind her, the coldness and rough texture drawing his thoughts from inappropriate cravings.

"Pitt," she whispered.

He looked down into her beautiful green eyes, softened with desire. "Aye?" Sunlight shimmered on her auburn-colored hair and encircled her head like a crown of light.

"Kiss me…like before."

Anguish threaded into her voice. An answering ache gripped his heart, a wish for much more between them than a few stolen kisses, but she'd told him weeks ago of her betrothal. Her fate couldn't be changed, no matter how much they wanted it to be.

Here in this ancient place, though, she was his. He could imagine, in this spot where countless lovers must have kissed before, that she belonged to him—and always would. He lowered his mouth to hers again. As she arched against him and clung to him, he swept his tongue into her mouth. Today, he'd leave his mark upon her heart; his invisible claim that if things had been different, or ever could be different, they'd be together forever.

"Pitt," she half-whispered, half-moaned.

Closing his eyes, he kissed her with all of the passion raging within him. As their lips brushed and molded together, he silently told her that he loved her. He always would. No other man would ever cherish her as sincerely and deeply he did.

As she wilted against him, voices carried on the wind.

"Aye, 'tis true," a man said in a raised voice. "Our mates'll deny it, but 'tis the truth."

The guards.

Pitt broke the kiss. Blythe swayed toward him; he caught her arms, steadying her.

Her expression dazed, her cheeks flushed and strands of her hair caught on the stone behind her, she stared at him. He'd never seen a more beautiful woman.

"Right yourself," he murmured.

She blinked, her gaze still unfocused.

"The guards," he said, more urgently.

The dreaminess left her expression. Straightening, she swiftly smoothed her hair and cloak. As she hurried from the shadows of the monolith into bright sunlight, the two guards strode into view.

As though she'd been studying the stone directly ahead of her, her attention shifted from it. Her expression calm and collected, she met Pitt's gaze. "Thank you. I am grateful for what you shared with me."

"My pleasure, milady." He fought not to grin.

"I should return to the castle now. Would you please accompany me back to the fortress?"

Five days later

"If you have left any of your belongings behind, we will send them on to you."

"Thank you." Blythe smiled at the elegant and ever-gracious Lady Odelia Montgomery, who had become like a second mother to her. When Blythe dried her tears with a linen handkerchief, a raindrop landed on her hand, the beginnings of the rainfall the gray morning sky had promised.

Beside her, the door to the enclosed wooden carriage stood open. In the bailey beyond, tack jingled, and horses pawed the ground as the guards who would be safeguarding her on the journey waited for her to finish her goodbyes. Once she stepped inside the vehicle, her life as Lord Montgomery's ward was over. She'd journey back to her father's castle, and in less than a sennight, she'd be married.

Her heart hurt, the pain greater than any she'd experienced before. If only she could have one wish fulfilled this Christmas: to spend the rest of her life with Pitt. They were destined to be together. She knew that with absolute certainty. But, when she'd sobbed in his arms, begged for them to run away together, he'd refused. Stroking her hair, his voice heavy with sadness, he'd told her the dream could never be.

"'Tis for the best," he'd murmured. "You deserve more than I can give you."

Tears trailing down her cheeks, her ladyship drew Blythe into her embrace. "I am not good at such moments."

Blythe hugged her ladyship. "Nor am I."

Lady Montgomery drew back to arm's length. "Come visit us whenever you wish."

Stocky, broad-shouldered Lord Montgomery, standing beside his wife, drew Blythe into his fond embrace. She blinked hard before turning to Rosetta. Her dear friend's eyes were red and puffy from crying. When their gazes met, Rosetta launched herself at Blythe.

"I do not want you to go."

Hugging her friend tightly, Blythe barely held back sobs. "You know I must."

"Promise you will write to me. Once a sennight, at least."

"Of course, I will."

Drawing back, Rosetta wiped her eyes. "At least I will see you soon at your wedding."

Days ago, they'd gone to their favorite spot in the garden; to the stone bench near the rows of grape vines that had gone dormant until Spring. She and Rosetta had spread a blanket on the bench and had sat and talked about their squires. Promising to attend each other's weddings had been one of the pacts Blythe and Rosetta had made to one another. At Blythe's nuptials, with lots of guests to speak with, she and Rosetta might not get much of a chance to talk to each other, but 'twould be wonderful to see her and her parents amongst the throng.

Blythe's vision cleared of tears for the barest instant—enough to recognize the man standing at the well, rinsing mud from his boots.

Pitt.

His gaze locked with hers. The anguish in his expression echoed the pain within her, and she fought not to wail. A low moan escaped.

Unable to bear any more, Blythe spun, stepped up on the mounting block and climbed into the carriage's shadowed interior. The dark wooden walls, as suffocating as a stone tomb, closed in on her.

Pressing her hand over her mouth, she fought not to collapse in a sobbing heap.

Her gaze fell to the opposite leather-covered seat, lit by sunlight. A folded piece of parchment, topped by a stone the size of a plum, lay there. Leaning over, she picked up the rock: It appeared to be a piece of the standing stones. With a shaking hand, she opened the parchment.

I love you. Never forget me.

A cry wrenched from her.

The carriage door closed, plunging her into near darkness.

Men called to one another outside, and the carriage jostled and started forward. Blythe fell on her side and wept.

Read the rest of Blythe and Pitt's Christmas adventure in *An Outlaw's Desire* by Catherine Kean.

About Catherine Kean

Award-winning author Catherine Kean's love of history began with visits to England during summer vacations, when she was in her teens. Her British father took her to crumbling medieval castles, dusty museums filled with fascinating artifacts, and historic churches, and her love of the past stuck with her as she completed a B.A. (Double Major, First Class) in English and History. She went on to complete a year-long Post Graduate course with Sotheby's auctioneers in London, England, and worked for several years in Canada as an antiques and fine art appraiser.

After she married and moved to Florida, she started writing novels, her lifelong dream. She wrote her first medieval romance, *A Knight's Vengeance*, while her baby daughter was napping. Catherine's books were originally published in paperback and several were released in Czech, German, and Thai foreign editions. She has won numerous awards for her stories, including the Gayle Wilson Award of Excellence. Her novels also finaled in the Next Generation Indie Book Awards, the National Readers' Choice Awards, and the International Digital Awards (twice).

When not working on her next book, Catherine enjoys cooking, baking, browsing antique shops, shopping with her daughter, and gardening. She lives in Florida with two spoiled rescue cats.

Connect With Catherine

Catherine loves to keep in touch with her readers!

Newsletter sign-up
https://landing.mailerlite.com/webforms/
landing/g8a7w8

Website
www.catherinekean.com

Facebook
https://www.facebook.com/Catherine-Kean-Historical-
Romance-Author-196336684235320/

BookBub
https://www.bookbub.com/profile/catherine-kean

Goodreads
https://www.goodreads.com/author/show/
695820.Catherine_Kean

Amazon Author Page
https://www.amazon.com/Catherine-
Kean/e/B001JOZEMU/

A Knight's Vengeance

Knight's Series Book 1 By Catherine Kean

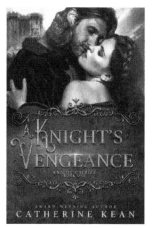

Geoffrey de Lanceau will never believe his father was a traitor. Back from Crusade, Geoffrey has vowed to avenge his sire's killing and reclaim the de Lanceau lands. When Geoffrey rescues a headstrong damsel from a near-accident and learns she's the daughter of his enemy, Geoffrey knows just how he will exact his revenge.

Lady Elizabeth Brackendale dreamed of marrying for love, but is promised to a lecherous old baron. Then she is abducted and held for ransom by a scarred, tormented rogue. He's the hero who saved her life. He's also the knight who intends to slay her father.

Elizabeth is determined to escape and undermine Geoffrey's plans for revenge, but the threads of deception sewn years ago bind the past and the present. When her father declares war, she's torn between her loyalty to him and her feelings for Geoffrey. Only by Geoffrey and Elizabeth championing their forbidden love can the truth at last be revealed about a knight's vengeance.

ISBN-10: 1092509747
ISBN-13: 978-1092509749
eBook ASIN: B006NQQ464

Dance of Desire

By Catherine Kean

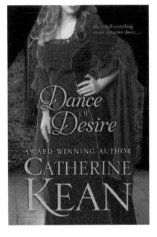

She risked everything in one seductive dance . . .

Disguised as a veiled courtesan, Lady Rexana Villeaux dances for Fane Linford, the new High Sheriff of Warringham. Desperate to distract him while her servant steals the missive that condemns her brother as a traitor to the Crown, she entices Fane with all the passion in her soul—and he is tempted.

A hero of the crusades, Fane has been granted an English bride by the king. Fane wants only one woman: the exquisite dancer. When he discovers she's actually a highborn lady, and that her rebellious brother is imprisoned in his dungeon, he will have no other wife but her.

Rexana doesn't want to become the sheriff's bride, but it may be the only way to save her brother. Yet as she learns more about her brooding husband tormented by barbaric secrets, she finds it harder and harder to deny his love or their dance of desire.

ISBN-10: 1479342890
ISBN-13: 978-1479342891
eBook ASIN: B005JRZF0Y

One Knight in the Forest

By Catherine Kean

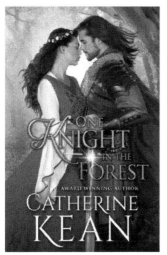

When Lady Magdalen Suffield finds a letter ordering her best friend's husband to commit murder, she flees into the woods. Pursued and injured, she collapses into the strong arms of Lord Cynric Woodrow, the local sheriff.

As Cyn treats her wound in his forest home, he wonders why she's running from a man he considers an honorable friend. She refuses to confide in Cyn, but as his fascination with her grows, he must choose between loyalty to her or to his friend. Can Magdalen win his trust and stop the murder, or will the danger destroy far more than the love Cyn and Magdalen seem destined to share?

ISBN-10: 1542330742
ISBN-13: 978-1542330749
eBook ASIN: B01MZ2IJXW

A Knight to Remember

By Catherine Kean

When widowed Lady Aislinn Locksmeade finds a naked, unconscious man in the forest, she wonders if he's Hugh Brigonne, her first and only true love. When he wakes, he can't remember who he is or what happened to him.

Does she dare to love the roguish stranger, or is there far greater danger to Aislinn than risking her heart?

ISBN-10: 1508409528
ISBN-13: 978-1508409526
eBook ASIN: B00UI68T8Q

That Knight by the Sea

By Catherine Kean

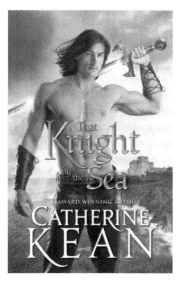

Lady Adaline Mortimer never expected to see Garrett Thurlow, the rebellious young lord she loved and lost, ever again. Yet, when she's kidnapped and held captive, the dark secrets of the past return.

In the cave of St. Agnes, will she and Garrett win a second chance at true love, or will they perish just like the legendary lovers before them?

ISBN-10: 1978170734
ISBN-13: 978-1978170735
eBook ASIN: B075ZHGX3H

A Legendary Love

By Catherine Kean

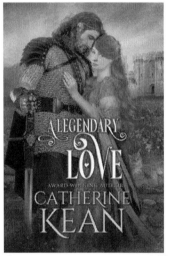

Tavis de Rowenne doesn't believe in curses. However, when a freak accident almost causes Lady Helena Marlowe, his intended, to drown, he wonders if his ancient cloak pin just might be damned.

Helena vows never to see or speak to Tavis again, but when her father falls ill, Tavis might be the only one who can save him. Does she dare to trust the roguish Scot with dangerous secrets, especially when he's determined to win her heart?

ISBN-10: 1537322257
ISBN-13: 978-1537322254
eBook ASIN: B01L4CWJCE

A Knight and His Rose
By Catherine Kean

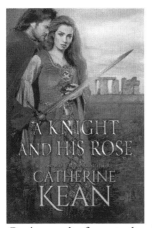

Wanting a few moments alone to gaze at the stars, Lady Violetta Molineaux sneaks onto the estate of her enemy, Lord Osric Seabrook, to reach an ancient stone circle. There she's discovered by a bold knight, but convinces him she's a commoner and hurries away, only to fall into a mysterious underground tunnel on Seabrook lands.

Osric can't forget the beautiful woman he met at the ancient site. Could she be Violetta? He'd met her years ago but not since his return from Crusade. When he finds her trapped and hurt in the tunnel he didn't even know about, he rescues her and takes her to his castle. He soon confirms her identity but plays along with her ruse of being common-born. Yet, when shocking secrets are unearthed in the tunnel, Violetta must tell Osric who she really is—and they both must acknowledge generations-old truths that will change their lives forever.

ISBN-10 : 1798647001
ISBN-13 : 978-1798647004
eBook ASIN: B07NQ148WM

Made in United States
Orlando, FL
08 December 2021

11263545R10124